Race to the Rescue

SADDLE ISLAND SERIES #3

Race to the Rescue

Sharon Siamon

Edited by Kate Zimmerman
Proofread by Ann-Marie Metten
Cover photos by Alexander Hafemann/iStockphoto (island)
    and Tim Graham/Alamy (horse & rider)
Map by Marc Peters
Cover and interior design by Jacqui Thomas and Five Seventeen
Typeset by Jesse Marchand

Printed and bound in Canada.

Library and Archives Canada Cataloguing in Publication

Siamon, Sharon
    Race to the rescue / Sharon Siamon.
(Saddle Island ; 3)

ISBN-13: 978-1-55285-855-4
ISBN-10: 1-55285-855-3

    I. Title. II. Series: Siamon, Sharon Saddle Island ; 3.

PS8587.I225R33 2007   jC813'.54   C2006-904983-1

The publisher acknowledges the financial support of the Canada Council
for the Arts, the British Columbia Arts Council, and the Government of
Canada through the Book Publishing Industry Development Program
(BPIDP). Whitecap Books also acknowledges the financial support of the
Province of British Columbia through the Book Publishing Tax Credit.

Please note: Some places mentioned in this book are fictitious while
others are not.

ANCIENT FOREST
FRIENDLY

The inside pages of this book are 100% recycled, processed chlorine-free
paper with 40% post-consumer content. For more information, visit
Markets Initiative's website: www.oldgrowthfree.com.

❧ **To Claire** ❧

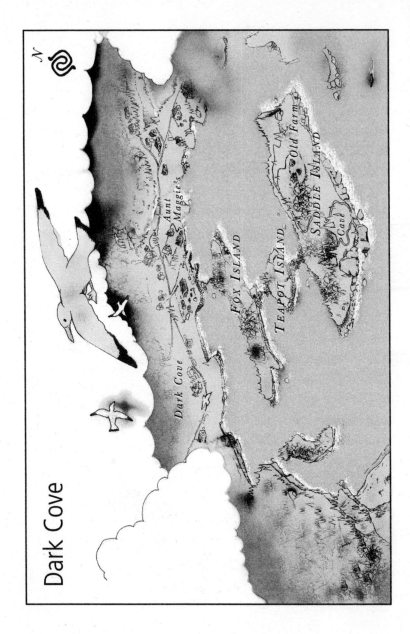

Contents ☷

Strange Call 🐚

There was no time to go and meet the woman who had called about the horse.

Kelsie MacKay had promised her dad she'd go straight home after school. But the woman from the Racehorse Rescue Society had sounded desperate on the phone that morning. She had a young mare who was going to be put down, unless Kelsie could take her.

"I'm calling on my cell," the woman had said. "I'll be passing Dark Cove around four-thirty. I could meet you at the old riding stable on the main road."

"I have to do it," Kelsie said out loud as she raced to the barn behind her Aunt Maggie's blue house. She slipped a bridle over the nose of her horse, Caspar, and climbed onto his wide, strong back. "We're going to see about saving another horse," she told him "—a little filly from the race track. So pretend you're a racehorse and gallop up the hill. Let's go!"

Caspar, as usual, seemed to understand. He gave one

hopeful glance at the ocean—Caspar loved to swim—but Kelsie leaned forward and spoke firmly in his left ear. "Not today, big guy."

She rode him bareback through the bushes behind the old barn, along a narrow path that snaked between the rocks, through a thick stand of black spruce, up to the main road that ran along the ridge above Dark Cove.

If only she wasn't too late. She hardly noticed the sun sparkling on the blue water, the green islands dotting the cove. The view had become familiar over the past two months. After spending her first thirteen years in a string of mining towns across Canada's north, Kelsie felt as if this Nova Scotia fishing village on the Eastern Shore was home.

Once on the road, Caspar broke into a smooth-flowing canter, covering ground with amazing speed. In no time, Kelsie had reached the cap gate over the Harefield Farms driveway.

There was no sign of a truck or horse trailer. "I've missed her," Kelsie groaned, yanking her auburn curls back from her face in frustration. "I should have promised to meet her instead of saying I'd try." The woman had made it clear that Kelsie had just this one chance to save the horse.

Kelsie rode over the bare, rubble-strewn stretch of gravel where the riding school barn had once stood and slid from Caspar's back. Earlier that summer, Paul Speers, a rich Bostonian, had torn down the barn to build a stud farm for racehorses. Maybe that's how the rescue society heard about us, Kelsie suddenly thought. Maybe they know Paul.

Just then Caspar gave an excited whinny. A truck was speeding up the drive. It crunched to a halt beside Kelsie. The truck was brown, with red lettering on the door that read RACEHORSE RESCUE SOCIETY.

Kelsie noticed a slim, aristocratic-looking horse's nose poking out of the trailer's window. She'd never seen such a bright, eager eye as the one turned toward her, or such finely sculpted features.

Caspar clearly felt the same way. He sidled up to the trailer, bobbing his head in greeting.

Meanwhile, a thin young woman had climbed out of the truck's cab. She wore a baseball cap pulled low over her eyes. "This is Diamond," she said, indicating the horse with a brief nod of her head.

"She's lovely," Kelsie gasped, her green eyes wide. "Why—why would anyone want to get rid of her?"

"She's no good coming out of the starting gate, and too slow for a racehorse." The woman's face was pale under the peak of her cap. She pulled a pack of cigarettes out of her vest pocket and lit up. "I don't have much time." She puffed smoke over her shoulder. "Can you take her?"

"You mean now? Right here?"

"Yeah. Sorry. I have to get to Truro by seven and pick up another horse." The woman shrugged. "That's how it is in this thoroughbred rescue business, one crisis after another."

Kelsie couldn't take her eyes off Diamond's soft eyes and slender muzzle. The mare had a small, diamond-shaped star on her forehead. Kelsie couldn't wait to see the rest of her.

"All right," she breathed quickly. "I'll take her."

"She's a five-year-old." The woman threw the rest of her cigarette on the gravel and ground it out with her heel. "Easy-going, most of the time."

That meant Diamond could be trouble, Kelsie knew. What would the mare do when they opened the trailer door and tried to unload her?

But Diamond backed out daintily, turned and touched noses with Caspar. Although they were almost the same height, the big white horse looked like a monster beside Diamond. Caspar had some workhorse in his ancestry. He was heavily built with sturdy legs and furry fetlocks around his big hooves. Diamond's legs were long and slender and didn't look strong enough to hold up the rest of her. She nudged Caspar playfully and he backed up against the truck, letting her be the boss. Right away, Kelsie could see the two horses were going to be friends.

"Got to go." The woman handed Diamond's lead rope to Kelsie. "Can you take her from here?"

"Sure." Kelsie took the rope and led Diamond and Caspar away from the truck. "We'll be fine." It wasn't as if the rescue society lady had given her any choice!

"Good. We'll be in touch about the paperwork."

The woman got back in the cab, slammed the door and started her engine. She didn't roll down her window to say goodbye to Diamond.

"Why is she so cold—doesn't she care?" Kelsie asked herself as the rig rolled away. "Or maybe she cares too much and tries to hide it?" Somehow, Kelsie doubted that. The woman didn't seem like a horse person. It was the cigarette. Fire was such a hazard in a barn that hardly anyone smoked around horses.

Keeping a firm grip on Diamond's rope, Kelsie climbed on Caspar's bare back. This was going to be tricky. She couldn't go fast on the road, holding Caspar's reins in one hand and Diamond's rope in the other. And she couldn't go back through the short cut to Aunt Maggie's. Going that way, through the woods and over the rocks, there were a hundred things to spook a strange horse.

Kelsie glanced at her watch. Almost five! Her dad was going to skin her alive. He'd be driving Aunt Maggie home from the hospital any minute.

"Don't fuss over your aunt," he'd told her and her twelve-year-old brother, Andy, that morning. "She'll be tired after the trip and weak from the heart surgery. Your job will be to keep things calm and quiet for Maggie. No surprises. No shouting or roughhousing. I want everything peaceful. You got that?"

Kelsie had been so glad when her father arrived from the Yukon after Aunt Maggie got sick. She had thought things would be better with Dad around. But it hadn't worked out that way. He'd been mad about something since the minute he'd walked through Aunt Maggie's door. Worse, she'd got used to making her own decisions since her father had left them with Aunt Maggie two months ago. Now she had to ask him before doing anything, and he usually said no.

Still, she'd promised to be quiet and helpful once Aunt Maggie got home. She loved her great aunt Maggie Ridout. And Kelsie was sure that worrying about her and Andy out in storms on the ocean hadn't helped her aunt's bad heart!

Aunt Maggie had lost her sister and brother-in-law, Kelsie's grandparents, in a storm off Saddle Island years before. She hadn't wanted Kelsie and Andy to go near Saddle Island. But it had drawn them both like a mermaid's song.

That's where Kelsie had hidden Caspar after she rescued him from Harefield Farms. And where Andy had found pirate treasure along the rocky shore. As for their friend, Jen Morrisey, Saddle Island had been her favorite place to paddle in her sea kayak. "And that's where we'll take Diamond," Kelsie thought as she made her way down the steep road to Dark Cove.

Diamond would live with Caspar and the three other horses from Harefield Farms at the old Ridout place on the island. There'd be five horses now—almost a herd.

Kelsie could hear a car coming up behind them. How would Diamond react? She slid from Caspar's back and pulled the mare behind his sturdy bulk to let the car pass. Caspar wasn't spooked by cars. Kelsie stood at their heads, waiting for the car to swoop by down the hill.

Instead, it stopped.

"Kelsie?" she heard her father ask. "What are you doing here? With Caspar? And that other horse?"

2

Racehorse @

It was her Aunt Maggie's car. Her dad was driving.

Kelsie struggled to keep hold of Diamond as the mare spun to face the car. Diamond was spooked—the car must have reminded her of a starting gate. She scooted forward and Kelsie had to let go of Caspar to catch up. "Easy!" Kelsie soothed, trying to calm her own thudding heart. This was no time for Diamond to lose it. Aunt Maggie didn't need any more frights.

"I thought you'd be home making sure everything was ready," Kelsie heard her dad mutter. She could tell he was trying to keep his voice level, but underneath a volcano was ready to erupt.

"It's . . . it's a long story, Dad. I'll be home in a minute. Hi, Aunt Maggie."

"Hello, dear." Her aunt was leaning out the back window. Her iron-gray hair was pulled back with two silver clips, as usual. Her face was gaunt after her stay in the hospital. But her eyes had a familiar glint as she took in Kelsie and the two horses. "Let's go, Douglas," she told Kelsie's father. "I can't wait to be in my own house."

"All right." He glared out the window, his blue eyes icy cold. "But Kelsie knows—I'm sure she understands we can't have one more horse around the place."

"This one's not like the other horses, is she?" Aunt Maggie asked. Diamond stood facing the car. "She looks like a racehorse."

"She was," Kelsie said. "But she was too slow. They were going to take her to the meat auction. I-I rescued her."

"A racehorse! That's all we need." Kelsie could almost hear her father's teeth grind like the gears of her aunt's car as he put it in first.

The sudden grinding sound sent Diamond into flight. Jerking the rope out of Kelsie's hands, she ran as if she was on a racetrack, neck stretched out, tail flowing behind—straight down the road toward town. She was around the next bend before Kelsie gathered Caspar's reins, clambered on his back and took off after her, leaving her dad shouting from the car, "Be careful!"

There was no time to take care. Caspar was no racehorse. There was no hope he could catch the fleeing Diamond.

The town of Dark Cove had only one main road that ran straight down from the highway to the shore. The other roads were one-lane gravel streets, wandering up and down over rocky outcroppings with houses set back from the road.

"Come on, Caspar," Kelsie urged as they thundered through town. If Diamond didn't go off on a side street she would end up at the water's edge. Kelsie prayed there wouldn't be a car or a truck between her and the beach.

Caspar galloped past the town's restaurant, the Clam Shack, past the street that led to Jen's house, past the driveway to Aunt Maggie's blue house. Now there was just the ocean, dead ahead.

Kelsie looked for the head of a swimming horse out in the surf. No Diamond.

Then she saw her, at the far end of the beach, where the boulders began. The mare turned and faced the water, took a cautious step, stopped and snorted at the waves.

"She's spooked by the ocean," Kelsie told Caspar. "Come on, this is our chance to catch her."

Caspar thudded down the wet sand. He gave one longing glance at the breakers cresting on the sloping sand. He loved to swim, but he understood his job—he had to block Diamond's flight back down the beach. Kelsie rode him up to the mare, bent down and grabbed her rope.

"Thanks, buddy," she whispered in Caspar's ear. "I owe you a swim."

ᘛᘛᘛ

Aunt Maggie's blue house stood on the shore. A path connected it to a dock that stuck out into the cove. The house was built of wood beams and planks, covered with cedar shingles to withstand the worst storms and weather the Atlantic could hurl at it.

Behind the house was a small barn, left over from the

days when the Ridout family farmed this shore. Kelsie led both horses inside and put Diamond in a stall. The mare was a rich chestnut all over except for the small diamond between her eyes. If her run had tired her, she showed no sign of it. "I have to go," Kelsie told Diamond, stroking her silky neck. "Dad and Aunt Maggie need me. But don't worry, girl, we'll look after you, somehow."

Caspar, she put in crossties. "Might as well go face the music," she whispered in his ear. She had looked forward to Aunt Maggie getting out of the hospital and them all living in her blue house. She hoped this hadn't got everything off on the wrong foot.

Kelsie went through the back door into a large porch, once used as a summer kitchen. She could hear her father's voice from the kitchen. He sounded irritated. Kelsie crossed the parlor, wishing she could run up the steep flight of stairs to her small bedroom under the eaves. She sighed and straightened her shoulders. No use putting off the lecture she was going to get from Dad.

But as she came into the kitchen, all her father said was, "I'll talk to you later about that horse. Take this tray to your aunt."

After dinner and dishes, Kelsie went back to the barn to feed the horses. Andy followed her. "Why is Dad so mad . . . ?" he started to ask. When he saw Diamond, his cheeks got red and his short blond hair stood up in spikes. "Where did you get that horse?"

"I couldn't help it, Andy," Kelsie tried to explain. "This

woman from a rescue society called this morning. She heard about our horses on Saddle Island. She said Diamond was going to be put down and look at her—she's beautiful. A racehorse."

"And what are we going to do with a racehorse?" Andy screwed up his face doubtfully.

"Keep her on the island, with the other horses. She and Caspar are already best buddies."

Andy went over to look at Caspar in crossties in the middle of the barn. "What happened to this guy?" he asked.

Kelsie stepped out of Diamond's stall and shut the door. "Nothing happened to Caspar. Why?"

"He's bleeding. Look!" Andy pointed to a smear of scarlet near his tail.

Kelsie hurried over, peered at the red streak. "Easy, fella," she told Caspar, reaching out to touch it. The smear was sticky and thick. Kelsie stared at her finger, then sniffed it.

"UGH!" Andy's eyebrows shot up. "What are you doing?"

"It's not blood," Kelsie said. She wiped her finger on Andy's arm. "It's paint. Red paint. See?"

"Ugh," Andy said again. "How did Caspar get red paint on his rump like that?"

"I don't know. Wait a sec . . ." Kelsie stared at Andy, seeing not her grossed-out brother, but a brown truck with bright red lettering on its side. "He backed into the Rescue Society's truck when Diamond first got out of the trailer," she said. "The paint must have been wet."

"Weird!" Andy muttered. "Did you notice anything else about the truck?"

"Maybe," said Kelsie, hesitating. "I think it had a different license plate—not one from Nova Scotia. But I didn't pay attention."

"You never pay attention when there are horses around," sighed Andy. "Why did you have to get another horse now, when we're trying to make everything perfect so Aunt Maggie gets better and Dad stays with us in Dark Cove?"

"I know," Kelsie sighed. "But, Andy, if you could have seen that woman. She was so cold, I'm sure if I hadn't taken Diamond she would have driven her straight to the slaughterhouse."

Andy threw up his hands. "You can't rescue every horse in the world!"

"No," Kelsie said, "just the ones I come across. It was like I was meant to have Diamond. Everything will work out. She won't be any bother, once she's on Saddle Island with the other horses . . ."

She clapped her hand to her mouth suddenly. "Oh, help, Andy—the island! I promised Jen we'd meet her there once Aunt Maggie got settled. She must be waiting for us."

"We can't go now," Andy said, "because of this stupid horse."

"I know," groaned Kelsie. "But I wish there was some way to let Jen know."

3

Someone's Watching @

Jen paced the landing place on Saddle Island. She searched the sea for any sign of Andy's green skiff. He had promised to bring Kelsie here to help with the horses, once Aunt Maggie was home and settled. Was it possible Andy and Kelsie had forgotten her?

Totally possible, Jen admitted to herself. Already, in this first week of school, they were making new friends. She wasn't going to have Andy and Kelsie all to herself, the way she had since they'd arrived in July.

Kelsie was in grade eight, so Jen hadn't seen her since they'd said goodbye at the school door that morning. Andy was in her class, grade seven, but he was a celebrity in Dark Cove these days. All the kids wanted to meet the new guy who had found pirate gold in a cave on Saddle Island and to hear his story.

The grade seven class got out early on the first day of school. Jen's mom had picked her up and offered Andy a ride home, too. Side by side in the back of the car, Jen had tried to recapture the closeness she and Andy had shared. "I guess you'll be pretty excited to have your Aunt Maggie home from the hospital," she said, touching his hand lightly.

Andy had hitched himself a little away from her. "Yeah, but now Dad has to sleep in my room. Kinda tight in there," he grunted.

What had happened, Jen wondered. All summer Andy had griped about how much he missed his dad. Now his father was here, it was a different story. She shook her head, remembering how irritated and distant Andy had seemed on that car ride. Where was the shy boy who'd kissed her when they were trapped in a tunnel together? He didn't seem to remember that!

Andy had better hurry, if he was coming, Jen thought, scanning the channel between Saddle Island and its nearest neighbor, Teapot Island. The tide was falling, and soon the rocks between the islands would poke out, dangerous for a motorboat.

The landing place where she waited was a deep groove in the rocky shoreline of Saddle Island. It was just wide enough for a skiff or their friend Gabriel Peters' lobster boat. Jen's slender red sea kayak, the *Seahorse*, was pulled up to one side, looking like a crimson autumn leaf on the smooth gray rock.

The sun was sinking low over the mainland. It would be dark in an hour and a half. Jen couldn't wait any longer. She turned her back on the sea and headed toward the old Ridout farm, where the horses waited. Once, Andy and Kelsie's ancestors had lived on this island. There had been a house, a barn, gardens and hay fields. Now, trees grew over everything, closing in old paths and roadways until they were like tunnels through a matted forest.

Jen heard a sound to her right, like a stick snapping underfoot. She stopped, stood still, the silence of the forest ringing in her ears. She could hear the boom of waves on the shore. Overhead, seagulls screeched. Jen listened till her ears ached but heard no human sound. The crack of the stick must have been an animal.

She pressed on. The tunnel of trees ended at a small stone barn. This summer, they'd put a new roof on the barn, with Gabriel's help. Beyond the barn was a pasture, fenced with electric wire, fueled by solar panels. The fence zigzagged from tree to tree, and at the far end was a spring with a low stone wall around it.

The horses were gathered around the spring in the long evening shadows, but when they heard Jen approach they ran to the barn to greet her. Midnight was a plump, glossy Canadian mare, with a frizzy mane and a kind face. Sailor was a feisty Newfoundland pony who thought he was a big horse. And Zeke was a leggy quarter horse so relieved to be rescued from the tedious life of a school horse that his whole personality had changed. He galloped up to Jen, stopped on a dime and thrust his long brown nose into her pocket.

"Hey. You know I've always got a carrot for you, don't you?" Jen fed him the chunk of carrot off the palm of her hand.

"Did you guys wonder where we disappeared to this week?" She pulled out more carrots as the others gathered around. "We got stuck inside school walls, that's where. And this is only week one.

"You're so lucky that you don't have to worry about Harefield Farms and lessons anymore," she told the horses. "Although I sure could use the money I used to make at the riding stable."

Jen rested her forehead on Zeke's long face. "I gave Mom my share of the treasure money to pay bills and she still doesn't have a job," she said. "Everybody at school knows we're hard up—" That was the worst thing about living in a place with only a hundred people, Jen thought. Everybody knew everybody else's business.

Suddenly, Sailor gave a warning whinny. "What? Is Andy coming?" Jen whirled around. But there was no one in sight. "That's weird," she muttered, straightening Sailor's forelock, which, as usual, was in his eyes. "You thought you heard Andy, didn't you, boy?" The pony had exceptional hearing, and Andy was his favorite person.

Jen had a strange feeling that someone else was in the clearing. But who could it be? No one came to the island except the three of them and, occasionally, their friend Gabriel Peters. No one had come there for years, except her, to sit high up on a rock called the Saddlehorn on the island's north end. And then Kelsie and Andy had arrived. They had made Saddle Island a refuge for horses that no one wanted, a private island all their own.

So why would anyone be here now?

No time to think. All the horses needed her. "Take it easy," she scolded Sailor as he head-butted her while she groomed Zeke. "There's only one of me and three of you. I hope nothing's happened to Aunt Maggie and that's why Andy and Kel didn't come." She spoke louder, to show anyone who might be listening that she wasn't scared.

The horse chores took time. Zeke had a stone lodged in his hoof. Carefully, she dug it out with a hoof pick. Midnight had somehow got burrs tangled in her long mane. "Stand still!" she ordered as the mare tossed her head, "or your whole mane will be a matted mess! I'm sure Kelsie would be here to help if she could. Something must be wrong!"

Jen finished giving the horses their grooming and fed them each a scoop of grain to keep them happy. They were all right on their own, with grass in the pasture, water in the spring and shelter under the trees. Come cold weather or hurricanes and it would be a different story, but then they'd move them to Aunt Maggie's barn on the mainland for the winter.

As she closed the barn and gave Zeke a final pat, Jen once again felt eyes on her. Was someone watching from the forest—waiting for her to leave?

"I'm just spooked because I'm here by myself," she told Midnight. "You look after these guys, won't you? You're the boss, while Caspar is away." The horses had a pecking order. Caspar was at the top and Sailor was at the bottom. Caspar had been known to get the rest of them in trouble, breaking through the electric fence to get to the ocean for a swim, but Midnight was steady and reliable.

"I've got to go," Jen said, as though she was announcing it to someone listening from the trees.

The prickly sense of being watched stayed with her as she ran down the overgrown road to the landing. She felt relieved to shove her kayak into the shallows at the narrow end of the glacial groove and climb aboard. She reached for her paddle, held in place by bungee cords that crisscrossed the top of the hull.

With the tide out, the water was low but the kayak had no problem navigating the shallow waters between Saddle and Teapot islands. Jen spun through the rocks, surfing on the waves that swirled around them until she was out in the deeper water of the cove. She looked back. The shore of Saddle Island was as empty and lonely as ever. So why did she feel there were still those eyes watching her paddle away?

Night Lights @

Later that night Kelsie lay in bed, too worried and excited to sleep. A new horse! But Dad said they couldn't keep her. She'd have to change his mind about that! If only they could get Diamond over to Saddle Island—he'd see she wasn't any trouble.

She wished she could share her problems with her friend, Jen. She hadn't been home when Kelsie called at eight. Probably still working on Saddle Island, doing the horse chores all three of them should have been doing.

Kelsie tossed in her narrow iron bed and kicked at her heirloom quilt. Her small room had a plank floor, slanted ceilings and a stunning view of the sea. Andy and her father slept in an identical room across the hall.

If she could just fall asleep! Her father had stayed mad all evening and there had been a thousand things to do getting Aunt Maggie settled. When it was all done, Kelsie had gone to bed. She wanted to get up at five to see to Diamond before making breakfast and heading for school. Then Dad couldn't complain.

She heard a small sound downstairs. Waited . . . heard it again. Kelsie kicked off her quilt and swung her bare feet to the floor. She tiptoed quickly down the narrow stairs to the kitchen, where she could see a light on.

Aunt Maggie was in her long white nightgown, leaning on the kitchen sink. "I was trying to get a glass of water," she said.

"I'll get you one. Let me help you back to bed," said Kelsie. Aunt Maggie's legs were just two stick shadows through the thin cloth. Kelsie tried not to look, or to feel how weak her aunt's arms felt as she helped her back to the sun porch.

"Thanks. I wasn't sure I could make it. Sorry I woke you up."

"Don't worry. I wasn't asleep." Kelsie tucked her aunt into bed.

"I'll bet you were thinking about your new horse . . . what's her name?"

"Diamond."

"She'll do fine. Don't worry about your father's fussing. He'll come round in a day or two."

Somehow, Aunt Maggie's sympathy made Kelsie feel worse than all her dad's scolding. Her aunt's pale face against the pillow and her hair fanned out around her head was so not like stern, strong Aunt Maggie that it was frightening.

"Thanks for understanding." Kelsie sat on the edge of the bed and tucked the quilt around her aunt's shoulders. "Don't worry about anything. Just work on getting better."

Aunt Maggie smiled a faraway smile. "That's what I intend to do. It's so nice having Douglas here again."

Aunt Maggie had brought up Kelsey's father after his parents drowned, but he hadn't lived in Dark Cove for many years.

There was a pause. "It's strange," Aunt Maggie went on. "This porch was first made into a bedroom for a sick person. I never thought I'd be lying here like poor Maude, too weak to get up."

"Who was Maude?" asked Kelsie.

"She was my great aunt." Aunt Maggie picked at her quilt. "I never knew her. But my grandfather told us her story every January when the weather was coldest. Maude was supposed to die of tuberculosis when she was eighteen, but her father, your great-great grandfather, insisted on bringing her home to Dark Cove from the sanatorium. He was sure the sea air would cure her disease. So he put her bed on this porch and she lay here while the winter winds blew and frost formed on her quilt and the water froze in her washbasin every morning."

"What happened? Did Maude freeze to death?" Kelsie said.

"No. She got better." Aunt Maggie smiled. "She lived to be a grown woman, married and had six children before she died."

"But then she died," Kelsie said.

"We all do." Aunt Maggie reached for Kelsie's hand. "Don't be sad, Kelsie. It's just strange. I've never been sick a day in my life and now I'm too weak to get up for a drink of water."

"Oh! Your water." Kelsie jumped up. "I'll get it." She brought Aunt Maggie a cold glass from the kitchen tap. "Can I bring you anything else?"

"No, I'll be fine now." Aunt Maggie reached for her pill bottle. She swallowed two white capsules and lay back with a sigh.

"I should let you rest," said Kelsie. "And I have to get up really early to look after Diamond, so I should go to bed, too."

"Just like my sister Elizabeth," her aunt murmured. Her gray eyes glowed with memory. "Always thinking of her horses. Having you here is like having her back. She used to come in at night, sit on the edge of the bed with her long auburn curls around her face—just exactly like yours." She reached up to twist one of Kelsie's curls between her fingers. "Elizabeth would talk about her horses," Aunt Maggie went on. "She knew I didn't care about those nags. She just wanted someone to talk to—couldn't keep all that excitement inside."

Kelsie shivered. It made her feel weird when her Aunt Maggie talked like this, as if Kelsie was her dead sister.

She leaned forward and kissed her great aunt's pale forehead. "Goodnight," she whispered. "The sea air will make you better, like Maude."

Her aunt closed her eyes. "Goodnight, Elizabeth," she whispered.

"I'm not . . ." Kelsie backed away from the narrow

white bed. She knew she looked just like her grandmother, Elizabeth Ridout. Same reddish brown hair and green eyes. The first time Aunt Maggie had seen her this summer she'd started like a spooked horse—like she'd just seen a ghost. It wasn't just looks. Aunt Maggie had it in her mind that Kelsie was wild like Elizabeth, stubborn and reckless and horse crazy.

Climbing slowly back to her room, Kelsie heard Andy start to snore and her dad mutter under his breath. Their bedroom was small for two people. It was a dream come true when Dad moved back to Dark Cove, she thought, but why did he seem so grumpy all the time?

She tossed and turned in her bed. How was she going to get Diamond to Saddle Island? Caspar, she could swim back there, but Diamond was afraid of water.

She thought about Gabriel Peters, who'd helped get the other horses to Saddle Island on his fishing boat, the *Suzanne*. Too bad Zeke had dented the *Suzanne*'s hull and pooped on her deck. Kelsie was sure Gabriel would say the same thing as Andy and her dad. "Not another horse!"

Thinking about Gabriel made her twist and turn under her quilt. Why did he have to be so irresistible with his dark curly hair and laughing brown eyes? He was four years older, as out of reach as the moon. Kelsie forced her tired brain back to the problem of Diamond. Maybe Jen would have some ideas. She knew everybody in Dark Cove.

☙ ☙ ☙

Meanwhile, Jen was sitting on her own bed, in a small house

not far away. Her mom, Chrissy, stood in the bedroom door. Her face was pale with anger. "I've warned you about kayaking after dark," she said. "One more time and that kayak is history."

"I said I was sorry." Jen glowered back at her mom. "But I know every speck of this shoreline. I can find my way after dark. Anyway, I couldn't help it. Andy and Kelsie didn't come to help with the horses. Zeke had a stone in his hoof. Midnight's mane was full of burrs. What was I supposed to do—just leave them like that?"

"I don't want to hear it." Jen's mom held up her hand. "I expect you to obey the rules." She paused. "I'm sure Andy and Kelsie were too busy to come. I hear Maggie Ridout is doing as well as can be expected, but she's weak after her operation. Kelsie has that new horse and . . ."

"What new horse?" Jen stared at her mother.

"Didn't she tell you? She bought a thoroughbred mare. Brought her home today. What she plans to do with a racehorse in Dark Cove I can't imagine."

Jen couldn't believe it. "Kelsie didn't say anything about a new horse. How could she not tell me?"

At the same time, she thought, it all fits. Kelsie doesn't care about me now school has started. She's too busy, all right—with new horses and new friends. No time to let me know what's going on.

"I'm not surprised," her mom was saying. "Maggie Ridout's family were always a bit above themselves—they used to own all the land around here. And Doug, Kelsie's dad, he was very stand-offish when we were in high school."

Jen could see her own feelings of being "not quite good enough" mirrored on her mom's face. It made her angry— Kelsie and Andy weren't like that. Or were they?

ଡ ଡ ଡ

In the middle of the night Kelsie woke up. At first, she thought it was morning. A beam of light streaked across her slanted ceiling. Then the light disappeared and she realized it was still pitch dark outside.

Kelsie sat up, rubbed her eyes and went to the window. She could see a light, way out at sea, past the islands. It must be a fishing boat sailing by, she thought. Strange, that light shining so brightly on her ceiling. She couldn't see the barn from this window, but everything seemed peaceful outside. "I must have been dreaming," Kelsie said with a yawn and went back to bed.

5

Kelsie Explains @

Kelsie crept downstairs before six the next morning. She used the bathroom without flushing, trying not to make any noise. "Please don't wake up," she silently begged her dad and Aunt Maggie as she tiptoed to the door. "Let me get to the barn to see my horses before you start asking me to do stuff for you."

Outside, the boom of the waves hitting the beach farther down the cove was like a song. It was just before sunrise. The air smelled fresh and salty. Kelsie took a deep breath and felt it right down to her toes.

As she opened the barn door and let in the dawn light, she heard Caspar shift restlessly in his stall. "Hi, big guy," she murmured, going over to stroke the long white nose that poked over the stall door. "You hate being stuck in there, don't you? Don't worry, I'll get you back to the island as soon as I can." She had swum Caspar over to the mainland two days ago to get his hooves trimmed.

A soft whinny came from the next stall. Caspar swung his

head around to look at Diamond blinking at him. "Did you tell her all about Saddle Island?" Kelsie laughed. "Tell her about the good grass and the cold spring water and the trail to the barn overhung with blackberry vines?" She was sure horses had a way of talking to each other that was as good as words.

Kelsie brought them each a bucket of clean water from the tap outside the barn and a flake of hay for their nets. "I have to go to school," she explained to Caspar as he munched hay with his big teeth, "but I'll run home at lunch to check on you. Meanwhile, you look after Diamond." She rubbed Caspar between his eyes and stroked his ears.

Diamond whickered softly. "Okay, you, too," Kelsie laughed, reaching over to stroke the mare's velvety nose. "I should muck out your stalls, but I have so much to do before school . . ."

"I could help," Kelsie heard a voice behind her say.

She wheeled around. "Jen! Where did you come from? What are you doing here?" She looked at her watch. "It's six-thirty in the morning." Jen's slender figure stood in the barn doorway, her straight, silky brown hair loose around her face.

"I-I couldn't sleep," stammered Jen. "I was worried when you didn't show up yesterday."

"I'm sorry!" Kelsie started to explain. "We couldn't come because . . ."

"I heard." Jen nodded. "Mom told me you bought a new horse."

"I didn't buy her, I rescued her. Come and see." Kelsie reached out her hand to Jen. "This is Diamond." She told Jen the story of the phone call and meeting the woman from the Racehorse Rescue Society.

"So you didn't know until yesterday afternoon that you were getting her?" Jen held out a palm for Diamond to sniff. "What did your dad and Aunt Maggie say?"

"That's the problem." Kelsie sighed. "Dad is furious with me, but he doesn't want to yell because it will upset Aunt Maggie. She's still pretty weak. She acts weird, gets me confused with her sister Elizabeth."

"No wonder you couldn't get away." Jen patted Diamond's perfect cheek.

"I tried to call you but you must have been on the island. Then it got too late and we all went to bed early because of Aunt Maggie." Kelsie paused. "I should go. See if she needs me."

"I'll muck out the stalls." Jen opened Diamond's stall door.

"Thanks." Kelsie gave Jen a grateful grin. "While you're at it, help me figure out how I can get her to Saddle Island. I'll see you at school."

@@@

Jen studied Diamond's beautiful young head. She'd never seen a thoroughbred up close. She did look different, proud and superior, with an elegant arched neck and large, glowing eyes.

Jen slipped into her stall and stroked Diamond along her withers and backbone. She must be well over sixteen hands, Jen thought. Diamond quivered at her touch, but soon lowered her head, letting Jen know she liked the gentle massage along her spine.

But when Jen's hand smoothed down her shoulder and over her ribs, Diamond snorted and moved away.

Jen gasped. "What's wrong? Does your stomach hurt? We should get the vet to check you out." She closed Diamond's stall and headed for the back door of the blue house to tell Kelsie.

Stepping into the back porch, she heard voices from the kitchen. Kelsie's and the voice of Andy's father, Doug, who was trying not to yell, but there was a fierce intensity in his voice that made Jen stop and back up.

"Where were you when your Aunt Maggie was calling?"

"I . . . was in the barn . . . feeding the horses," Jen heard Kelsie say.

"Horses! Don't you think I have enough trouble without you running off to play with your horses before breakfast?"

"I wasn't playing."

"I don't care what you were doing. I need you to help with Aunt Maggie. I'm counting on you. Do you understand?"

"Yes, but . . ."

"No buts. I want Caspar out of that barn and back on Saddle Island—like now!" Doug MacKay's voice was rising. "And as for that mare—I've told you—get in touch with those people who dumped her on you and get them to take her back!"

This wasn't a good time, Jen decided, to suggest calling the vet for Diamond. She ducked out of the porch and hurried back to muck out the stalls in the barn. It would have to wait until she saw Kelsie and Andy at school.

@@@

The school was a square stucco building at the far edge of Dark Cove. When Jen's mom had gone there, it had eight classes. Now there were barely enough kids to fill four classrooms, even with kids bused in from up and down the shore. The kids from kindergarten to grade two were in one class, grades three, four and five in a second. Jen and Andy were in a split grade six and seven. Kelsie and the other grade eights had a classroom to themselves. High and mighty seniors.

Jen waited on the wide front steps. Andy came first, surrounded by his new friends. He gave Jen a shy half-wave and hurried by her.

Ten minutes later, Kelsie tore across the schoolyard and up the steps. "Whew!" She took a deep breath and shook her head. "I am definitely not cut out to be a nurse. And every time Aunt Maggie sneezes Dad wants to call the doctor."

"Speaking of doctors," said Jen, "I think you should get Dr. Bricknell to check Diamond. She seems a bit touchy around her belly."

"I should," Kelsie agreed. "She needs to get checked out by a vet before she goes to the island—if I can figure out a way to get her there. My dad's still talking about getting rid of Diamond. I don't know what I'm going to do."

Just then, the morning bell shrilled. Kids streamed toward their classrooms. "I've got to go," Kelsie cried. "Ms. Stannard has a fit if we're late. I'll see you at noon." She took off, skidding down the hall, calling over her shoulder. "We'll talk to Gabe. Maybe he can help."

Jen watched her go. Good luck, she thought. They hadn't seen hunky seventeen-year-old Gabriel Peters since he started school. He'd be busy—he was such a hotshot—with the hockey team, school council, girls. If she knew Gabriel, Kelsie had her work cut out for her, asking him to help.

𝕢 𝕢 𝕢

"I don't want to look too obvious," said Kelsie, later that afternoon. She swung her backpack onto her other shoulder. The girls stood by the side of the main road, waiting for the high school bus. "Do you think it looks like we're waiting for him?" Kelsie asked Jen.

"He won't notice," Jen predicted. "And if he did, he wouldn't care."

The yellow school bus rolled down the narrow road toward them and stopped with its red lights flashing. Gabe got off last, after a group of giggling girls.

"Hi!" He waved to Kelsie and Jen through a screen of his admirers.

"Oh, look!" said a blonde girl, in a loud voice. "It's that red-headed kid with the crush on Gabriel. Isn't that cute? She came to meet the bus."

Kelsie recognized Steffi LeGrand. Talk about girls

with a crush on Gabriel! She practically draped herself all over him.

Now Steffi sidled up to Kelsie. She looked her up and down, as if Kelsie were a strange life-form. "I hear," she said loudly so her friends could hear, "that you've been in love with Gabriel ever since he pulled you off a rock before the tide swept you out to sea. Too bad it didn't."

"I heard she rode her bike in front of his truck just to get his attention," another of the girls chimed in. "It's pitiful, if you ask me."

"She wrecked his lobster boat ferrying horses to Saddle Island," Steffi said, eyes narrowing, "and then tried to crash our beach party."

Kelsie stared around the group of girls. Did everyone know about every single embarrassing moment of her first two months in Dark Cove? Apparently they did.

Jen grabbed her hand and towed her away. "C'mon. Let's get out of here."

Gabriel walked beside them, scowling, pretending he hadn't heard. But Kelsie could see that his ears were red. "What's up?" he asked.

Kelsie didn't have the nerve to ask him to take Diamond to Saddle Island. Not after that. "Not much," she murmured. "How about you?"

"Oh, you know. Just school." He grinned, and the scowl that had darkened his face disappeared. "It's good to see you kids. How's Andy? How's his boat?"

"Fine." Kelsie gulped. She had to think of something

else to say. "Speaking of boats, I saw a light way out beyond Saddle Island last night," she told him. "Do people fish at night?"

Gabriel's frown was back on his handsome face. "Tell me more," he said. "Was the light steady, or did it flash?"

"I-I'm not sure," Kelsie faltered. "I didn't watch it very long. Why?"

"There's a lot of drug smuggling along this coast," Gabe said. "Sometimes a boat lies offshore and signals that it's ready to land a shipment."

"Drug smuggling?" Kelsie turned to Jen. "Did you know about this?"

Jen nodded. "Everybody knows."

"Did you see any answering light from the shore?" Gabe asked.

"I don't think so." Kelsie remembered the flash of bright light that had woken her from a sound sleep. "Maybe. I saw a light on my ceiling, but just for a second."

"If you see it again, tell your dad, or me," said Gabriel. They had reached the lane to his house. He paused. "Give my best to Andy and your Aunt Maggie," he said. "See you around."

6

Diamond's Secret ◎

"You never asked Gabe about taking Diamond to the island," said Jen, as they turned and walked toward their houses on the other side of Dark Cove.

"How could I, after those girls. Why are they so mean?" Kelsie yanked at a tall weed by the side of the road. "Like poisonous snakes."

"They can see how you feel about Gabe. It's written all over your face," Jen told her.

"So? Like they all said, I'm too young for him."

Jen sighed. "I tell you, Gabriel Peters is like royalty in Dark Cove. Steffi's had her eye on him since kindergarten. She's got big plans."

She tried to explain. "Look, Kel, around here, if a lobster fisherman tries to poach on another lobsterman's fishing ground, they cut the lines to his traps, sink his boat or fill it with rotting fish. You're poaching on Steffi's territory—that's Gabriel."

"She doesn't own him!" Kelsie cried indignantly.

They had reached Jen's house. She paused before she went in. "Maybe not, but be careful," she warned. "You and Andy are new here. If Steffi and her friends think you're a serious threat, you're in trouble."

"But I'm not a threat, that's just it." Kelsie threw out her arms. "Gabe likes Andy because Andy's crazy about boats. He just puts up with me. He'd never take me seriously."

Jen gave her a sharp look. "Maybe not now. But four years is not that much when you're older—I'll bet that's what Steffi's thinking." She opened the front door. "Can you come in for awhile?"

"No." Kelsie shook her head. "Aunt Maggie might need me and the vet's coming—I called him at noon. Plus, I have to get Caspar ready to swim to Saddle Island tonight. Dad is so freaked—he'll feel better when at least one horse is gone."

"I'll take the kayak and go to the island with you," Jen offered. "And I'll do the horse chores if you need to get back to Aunt Maggie."

"Thanks." Kelsie grinned. "It's good to have a best friend to count on." Her grin faded at the look on Jen's face. "What's the matter?"

"I wasn't sure I was your best friend." Jen spoke directly, looking into Kelsie's eyes. "Since school started . . . I mean, I hardly see you."

Kelsie gulped. "Jen, have I been acting like a big shot?"

"Sort of. I know you've got new friends."

"But you're my best friend in the world."

"Does Andy feel the same way?" Jen's blue eyes were still direct.

Kelsie fumbled for an answer. "I can't speak for my little brother. But if he gives you a hard time, I'll sink his skiff."

"No!" Jen pushed the door open. "Don't say anything. We'll work it out. Meet you at the dock at six."

☙☙☙

Dr. Bricknell, the veterinarian, had a deeply lined face, white hair that he wore carefully brushed to one side, and stooped shoulders. He examined Diamond carefully, listening to her heart and belly sounds, feeling her muscles and joints. "Can't tell without an ultrasound, for sure," he murmured, "but my experience tells me this mare is pregnant."

He straightened up. "Looks like you rescued two horses instead of one."

Kelsie couldn't speak. She just stared at the vet.

"Didn't the rescue society inform you?" Dr. Bricknell asked.

Kelsie shook her head.

"Well, it's possible they didn't know—hard to be sure in the early months." He paused. "What did they tell you about this mare?"

"Just that . . . that she was too slow to race and nervous coming out of the gate," Kelsie managed to sputter.

"Didn't give you any documentation? Papers?"

Kelsie shook her head again.

"Or ask for a donation to cover costs, or get you to sign a contract?"

"N-no. It all happened too fast."

Dr. Bricknell lifted Diamond's lip and looked under it. "Here's her tattoo," he said. "All thoroughbreds have them. But without a contract or any money changing hands, I'm not sure that you own this little mare."

Kelsie's head was spinning. "The woman said she'd get back to me."

"And no doubt she will." Dr. Bricknell patted Kelsie's shoulder. "In the meantime, don't worry. The mare seems in very good shape, and if she is expecting a foal it won't be born until the spring. Just make sure she gets plenty of good grass, and later we'll talk about supplements to her diet."

@ @ @

That evening after dinner Kelsie sat on her Aunt Maggie's dock, waiting for Jen. She was wearing a wetsuit borrowed from Jen—it would be much better for riding a swimming horse than jeans and a sweatshirt. Caspar was on the lawn behind her, munching grass. His steady chewing calmed her racing thoughts.

The tide was coming in. Kelsie could hear all the sounds of the ocean: the splash and trickle of the waves in and out of the rock pools below the dock, the slap of the water on the dock's pilings and, farther off, the slow boom and hiss of waves hitting the Dark Cove beach and falling away again.

The kayak made almost no sound as Jen paddled up to the dock.

"Ready?" she asked.

"Even if I'm not, Caspar's so ready," Kelsie said. "This will be like a warm bath for him." Caspar loved to swim, even when the water was freezing, but now, in September, the ocean was the warmest it had been all year.

Kelsie tossed a bag of dry clothes to Jen to stow in one of the kayak's watertight compartments. "Can you take these over to the island for me?" she asked. "Andy's not coming till later to pick me up."

Jen caught the bag and twisted around to stuff it in the compartment behind her. As she did, her light brown hair hid the side of her face, but not before Kelsie saw the flush of hurt and disappointment that swept across it. Usually, Andy came to help with the horse chores. Poor Jen, thought Kelsie. What was the matter with Andy? She'd tried to talk to him about Jen. He'd promised to come down to the dock and act like a human being, but so far he hadn't shown up.

Kelsie sprang to her feet, ran to Caspar and led him to the water's edge. "I have something to tell you about Diamond," she called to Jen.

"Is it bad news?" Jen paddled closer. "Is she sick?"

"No, it's good news," Kelsie said, climbing on Caspar's broad back. "Dr. Bricknell thinks she's pregnant—going to foal sometime in the spring."

Jen let her paddle splash into the water in surprise. She reached forward to grab it. "I don't believe . . ."

"Shhh!" Kelsie warned as her brother came across the lawn. "Andy doesn't know about the foal yet."

"Hi," Andy said. He marched down the dock looking everywhere but straight at Jen and blushing to the roots of his spiky blond hair. "I wanted to make sure the skiff was ready to go later," he muttered, staring at his green motorboat as if it was the Cape Islander fishing boat of his dreams instead of a small skiff.

Kelsie leaned forward on Caspar's broad back. "And didn't you want to apologize to Jen for being such a jerk?" she suggested. "Go ahead, say you're sorry."

Andy looked from his sister to Jen, then raced away down the dock to his boat. Jen glared up at Kelsie. "You did say something to him. I told you not to!"

"I don't know what's the matter with him," said Kelsie. "Ever since Dad came he's been acting so funny. Not just to you . . ."

"Forget it!" Jen shook her head firmly. "Let's go. I promised Mom I'd be back before dark." She didn't look at Andy as she paddled past.

Caspar splashed joyously through the shallow water and then swam with strong, eager strokes toward the nearest island.

Kelsie loved the feeling of riding a swimming horse. His powerful muscles surged under her as they approached the shore of Fox Island. "He doesn't want to stop," she called to Jen in her kayak. "I'm going to swim him straight for Teapot Island. It will save time."

The three islands—Fox, Teapot and Saddle—had once been joined to each other and the mainland by a series of causeways. Fifty years ago, a monster storm had washed the roads away, tumbling the boulders that formed them as if they were bits of gravel. The rocks still lay in the shallow water between the islands, and at low tide they stuck up like rows of jagged teeth.

But now, with the tide coming in, stretches of blue sea separated the three islands. Fox was long and skinny, like a fox with a long tail. Teapot Island was just a bald dome of granite with one tree on top. Saddle Island, much larger than the other two, lay the farthest out to sea. It was saddle-shaped—high at both ends and low in the middle.

To get there, Kelsie swam Caspar around the south end of Fox Island and across the channel to Teapot Island. He splashed ashore, water streaming from his white mane and tail, snorting with annoyance.

"Don't worry, we're going back in the ocean," Kelsie said with a laugh. "One more channel to cross and you're home." Soon she was riding him into the groove in the rock that formed the natural landing place on Saddle Island's western shore.

"Come on, Caspar," Kelsie said, urging him out of the water. "Let's go find your buddies. I guess Jen went ahead without me—I goofed, trying to patch things up between her and Andy. Why do I bother? He's not good enough for Jen."

Caspar tossed his head as if to agree.

Jen's red kayak was already pulled up on the rocks. Kelsie

slipped from Caspar's dripping back, dug her clothes out of the kayak and changed behind a bush. She stuffed the wetsuit back into the kayak's compartment and climbed back on Caspar.

Before heading down the grassy track to the farm, the big white horse stopped, looked back toward the mainland and let out a loud whinny.

"Are you calling Diamond?" Kelsie leaned forward and stroked his wet neck. "Don't worry. We'll get her over here, somehow. That's one thing I can't goof up!"

7

The Clam Shack @

To Kelsie's and Jen's surprise, Andy came racing toward the farm an hour later, calling for Kelsie.

"You've got to come quick!" he shouted. "Diamond is kicking down her stall without Caspar. Dad's so mad—she's making Aunt Maggie crazy. She's sure Diamond is going to wreck the barn." He stopped and glared at his sister. "You and your horses—you always make trouble!"

Kelsie said. "All right. I'm coming. You okay to finish up by yourself, Jen?"

"Sure." Jen nodded. "And hurry. It's dangerous for Diamond to get so upset when she might be pregnant."

Andy stared from Jen to his sister. "WHAT?" His hair seemed to stand on end. "She's going to have a baby?"

Kelsie corrected him. "A foal," she said.

"Dad's going to have a dinosaur when he finds that out!" Andy shook his head. "Didn't the rescue society tell you when you took her off their hands?"

"Not a word." Kelsie said. "But it doesn't matter now. If

we can just get her here, she'll calm down. She wants to be with Caspar. Horses bond that way sometimes."

"Well, she'd better behave, or Dad will make sure she never sees Caspar again," Andy warned. He turned and marched away, back toward the landing.

"Sorry I blabbed about the foal," Jen said.

"It's all right," said Kelsie. "Andy was bound to find out."

Giving Caspar a quick farewell kiss on his nose, she hurried off toward the boat landing with her brother. "Bye, Jen," she called over her shoulder. "I hope you make it home before dark."

♨ ♨ ♨

Jen heard the distant growl of Andy's green skiff leaving the island. She made sure there was enough fresh hay for all the horses and the power was switched on for the electric fence. Then she hurried back to her kayak.

The sun was setting over the mainland, a huge orange fireball that turned the sea into a rainbow of color. Seabirds floated high above the island. Occasionally a tern dived for a fish, but it was a lazy time of night, the sea and the air calm before darkness descended.

Jen slipped her kayak into the water and grabbed her paddle. Time to go.

This time, she chose to paddle right instead of left. If the sea was calm it was faster to go home this way. Her route would take her to the north end of Saddle Island and then out into open water.

To Jen's surprise, she wasn't alone on the ocean. There was a kayak in front of her, slipping in and out among the rocks on the northwest corner of Saddle Island.

Lit by the setting sun, she could see the kayak was an odd camouflage green and brown, a large sea kayak, high at both ends. What was it doing out here? Solo kayaks were unusual on the ocean, especially at night.

Jen thought the paddler looked like a guy by the shape of his upper body. He had broad shoulders and powerful arms—but he was too far away to really see. He was probably a tripper, looking for a place to camp on the island.

She longed to follow him, but she knew she should get home. Jen had only about forty-five minutes before total darkness, and total trouble with her mom. She bent forward slightly, throwing her whole body into each stroke, and zoomed away from the island.

"I wonder if he sees me?" she muttered to herself, "and I wonder if he was here last night, when I felt someone watching me? I'd better tell Kelsie there's someone on the island, and Andy, too, if he cares."

Her kayak safely beached, Jen raced for home as darkness fell over the cove. Her mom was out and there was a note on the table to call Kelsie. Jen picked up the phone to call the blue house.

"Kel just left," Andy told her. "She went to the Clam Shack."

"Thanks," Jen replied. There was so much more she

wanted to say to Andy, but his voice was as tight as if he was talking to a stranger. She hung up the phone.

☙ ☙ ☙

The Clam Shack was Dark Cove's only restaurant. It was also an after-school hangout, a gossip center and the unofficial town hall. Jen and her mom had both worked there until that summer, when her mom went to work for Paul Speers, the rich guy who bought Harefield Farms. When he suddenly left town, she couldn't get her job back, and neither could Jen.

As she puffed up the steep slope from her house to the Clam Shack, Jen saw Kelsie hurrying up the longer path from her Aunt Maggie's.

Jen waited for her at the Clam Shack's front door. It seemed strange, she thought, not to dash in the back door, sling on an apron and go to work. "What are you doing here?" Jen asked as Kelsie reached the top of the path.

"There wasn't time to cook dinner after I got Diamond settled down, so Dad sent me for take-out." Kelsie gave Jen a weary grin. "She's got lots of spirit, that's for sure."

"Look who's here." Jen pointed to the counter as they opened the door and went in.

It was Gabriel, sitting alone on a counter stool. Steffi and her three friends sat around a table to one side of the restaurant. "I'm surprised his hair doesn't catch on fire, the way Steffi stares at the back of his head," Kelsie muttered as they walked past.

"Forget those girls. This is a perfect chance to ask Gabe about taking Diamond to the island." Jen nudged her arm. "Go on, you have to ask him sometime."

"All right, I'll ask." Kelsie slid onto a stool beside Gabriel, with Jen at her elbow.

"Hi." He turned with a grin. "What are you doing here?"

"Take-out for dinner," Kelsie told him. "It's crazy around our house. We've got this new horse . . ." She stopped to give her order to the waitress. "We'll have four lobster rolls to take out, with a large coleslaw and a bucket of clams."

Gabe dangled a fried clam from his bucket. "Look at these clams," he leaned past Kelsie to say to Jen. "Droopy, not crisp like they used to be when your mom was the cook. I hear the Clam Shack's for sale and might close down. No wonder, with food like this!"

Kelsie wondered desperately how to get off the subject of fried clams and back to Diamond.

Steffi did it for her. They heard her mocking voice from behind them. "Hey, Gabe, I see you're hangin' out with your horsey little friends again," she said. "Isn't it kind of late for them to be out on a school night?"

Gabe ignored her, but his eyes narrowed. "That's right— you have a new horse," he said to Kelsie. "Someone told me you rescued a thoroughbred that was going to the dog food factory. Is she giving you trouble?"

Kelsie didn't have time to answer. The Clam Shack door burst open. "Kelsie!" She spun on her stool to see her dad in the doorway. His face was knotted with worry and anger,

"Forget dinner. You've got to come home. Right now!"

"Is it Aunt Maggie?" Kelsie felt a jolt of fear.

"No. It's that fool horse," Doug MacKay said. "I thought you had it quieted down, but it's kicking like a wild thing— thumping around and making your Aunt Maggie anxious and upset. I promise you it's going back where you got it first thing tomorrow morning."

"But, Dad," Kelsie started, then realized everyone in the restaurant was staring at them. She could read sympathy on Jen's face, contempt on Steffi's and embarrassment on Gabe's. This was no place to be having a private argument. She gave the waitress a helpless shrug, got up and followed her father to the door.

It swung open in their faces as Jen's mom, Chrissy, barged through.

"Excuse me," she started to say, then looked up into Doug's startled face. "Hello, Douglas. It's been a long time since we've seen you in Dark Cove."

Kelsie's dad seemed frozen in the doorway. "I'm sorry— do I know you?"

"I guess not." Jen's mother's smile was twisted. "It's Christine Morrisey, big shot."

"Chrissy?" A shocked look spread over Douglas's face. "Now I remember. How are you? You look . . ."

"Old enough to be the mother of a twelve-year-old, I know." Chrissy gave a short laugh. "Come on, Jen, it's a school night. Time to be going."

There were giggles from Steffi and her friends. Doug was

still staring at Chrissy. "I was going to say you look exactly the same as you did in high school! It must be the sea air . . . or something."

"C'mon, Dad." Kelsie nudged his arm. "You said we had to go."

"Oh . . . yeah . . . we do. Emergency at home," Doug explained to Jen's mom.

"Your Aunt Maggie?" Chrissy looked worried.

"No, it's a horse."

Chrissy smiled. "Where Jen and Kelsie are concerned, it's always a horse."

"COME ON, Dad." Kelsie nudged him harder. The giggles from Steffi's table had turned into snorts of derision.

Jen watched them go. She hadn't had a chance to tell Kelsie about the stranger on Saddle Island. Oh, well, she thought, it isn't important. He'll probably be gone tomorrow.

She glanced at her mom. Chrissy was still watching Kelsie and her dad as they disappeared down the darkening path.

"So that's Doug MacKay," she said. "I'd have known him anywhere, and he didn't know me from a hole in the ground. Just like when we were kids."

"He remembered you, Mom," Jen said.

"That was just pretending. He hasn't changed."

8

Night Visitors

Back at the barn, Kelsie quieted Diamond again. "You have to stop kicking," she told the mare. "Your life is at stake. Yours, and your baby's."

Diamond turned her glossy rump to Kelsie. She was afraid Diamond would lash out with her rear hooves at the stall door. Instead the mare swayed restlessly, unhappiness twitching in every muscle.

"Stay quiet while I go get my sleeping bag and pajamas. I'm going to sleep in the barn with you tonight. Don't make a sound while I'm gone!" Kelsie warned.

As she headed up the stairs Aunt Maggie called from her sun porch, "Kelsie? Are you there?"

"I'm coming, Aunt Maggie." Kelsie hurried down the hall. "What can I get you?"

"Just sit here and talk to me," her aunt said. "Tell me, is that mare going over to the island?"

"Yes, as soon as we can get her there." Kelsie smoothed her aunt's covers.

"That's good." Aunt Maggie lay back and sighed. "She's an unhappy animal. I can feel it right through the barn wall and into this porch."

"She misses Caspar, Aunt Maggie," Kelsie said soothingly. "That's all."

"No!" Aunt Maggie sat straight up. "She's a badly frightened horse. I'm telling you that mare thinks something very bad is going to happen to her. Horses have a sixth sense."

Kelsie didn't think this was the time to tell Aunt Maggie that Diamond was expecting a foal, or that her dad was insisting they ship her back to the rescue society. "I'm going to sleep in the barn," she told her aunt. "I'll keep Diamond quiet."

"Thank you, dear." Her aunt's voice shook a little. "That's just what my sister Elizabeth would have done . . ."

"I'm not your sister!" Kelsie wanted to shout. Instead, she kissed her aunt goodnight and hurried away up the stairs to her room. Minutes later, arms full of bedding, she crossed the dew-soaked grass to the barn. It was fully dark now and out at sea she could see the same light as before. She stopped to look. Did the light flash? No, it was steady.

She slipped into the barn. Diamond stood in her stall, eyes wide, shivering. The light from the sea shone through the small window into her eyes. "Is that bothering you?" Kelsie said softly. "It's just a light. Gabe thinks it's drug smugglers, but it has nothing to do with us. We're going to settle down and sleep."

She didn't let herself think about what tomorrow might bring.

Half an hour later Kelsie heard soft tapping on the window of the barn. The door creaked slowly open. "Andy?" Kelsie asked, surprised at how loud her voice sounded. She pulled a chain, snapping on a light over the stall.

"No. It's Gabe." He came out of the shadows by the door.

Kelsie was so surprised to see him she couldn't breathe for a second. Gabe always had this effect on her, especially when they were alone. "What? Why . . . are you here?" she asked. She realized she was in her pajamas and her hair was probably full of straw.

"I stopped in to see your dad and your aunt Maggie," Gabriel said. "Your father seemed so upset in the Clam Shack—I was worried. Your aunt said you were out here. Thought you wouldn't mind if I came and said hello."

"I guess," Kelsie began, "sure. Come and meet my new mare." She pulled back her hair. She wasn't going to let Gabriel know how she felt!

He came closer and leaned his arms against the top of the stall door. "What's her name?"

"Diamond, like the jewel," said Kelsie.

"Quite a resemblance."

"What do you mean?" Kelsie threw up her head and at exactly the same second, Diamond did the same, ready for flight.

Gabe laughed. "She looks very smart, and she has dark reddish hair and a look in her eye that dares you to get in her way. I'd say she looks a lot like you."

"Don't make fun of her, Gabe." Kelsie stroked Diamond's shoulder. "She's only five years old and her life might be over before it's started. Dr. Bricknell thinks she's going to have a foal, and nobody wants the two of them, and Dad says I have to send her back to the rescue society. If you could have seen the woman who brought her! I always thought rescue societies loved horses, but she was as cold as a dead fish."

"Oh," Gabriel said. He moved closer and reached out a hand to Diamond. "Does your dad know about the foal?"

"No," Kelsie admitted, "and don't tell him. It would make things worse. He says I have to get her out of here. Tomorrow."

They were quiet for a moment. Kelsie watched Gabe stroke the mare's cheek with his large, strong hand. She drank in the sight of his rugged profile, his dark curly hair and wide shoulders, stifling a sigh. Gabe made all the other guys she'd met at school this week look like weedy kids. The stall door was between them, but he was so close . . .

"If I took her to the island on the *Suzanne*, would she be all right?" Gabe asked.

Kelsie jerked back to reality. "Uh . . . yes. Of course. But you said, after Zeke, there'd be no more ferrying horses on your boat."

"I'm not happy about it, but like your dad says, this is an emergency." A smile lit Gabe's face. "My dad's away, so he won't know. Meet me at our dock tomorrow after school— say five-thirty—and we'll see if we can get her across to the island."

Kelsie wanted to throw her arms around Gabe's neck, but instead, she hugged Diamond. "Thank you, Gabe."

"I don't mind going over to Saddle Island to check things out, anyway," Gabe said as he turned to go. "You haven't noticed anything weird, besides the light you saw the other night, have you?"

"N-no," Kelsie said. "But I haven't been to the island for the last few days, except to swim Caspar across. Jen's been doing all the chores. She hasn't mentioned anything."

"It still won't hurt to take a look around tomorrow," said Gabriel. "Sleep well, you two."

When he'd gone, Kelsie made herself a bed on clean straw and climbed into her sleeping bag. She thought about Gabe. You never knew if he was helping out because he liked you or just because he felt like doing something nice, or what was going on in that gorgeous head of his.

"Everything's going to be okay now," she promised Diamond. "I slept in here with Caspar when he was sick, so don't be scared. I'm here. And tomorrow, thanks to Gabriel, you'll be on Saddle Island."

Into the Ocean ◎

All the next day, the wind rose. By the time Kelsie led Diamond to Gabe's dock, whitecaps were lacing the dark water of the cove like frills on a velvet dress.

A stiff wind blew Diamond's forelock back from the white diamond on her forehead. She flared her wide nostrils and sniffed the sea wind as she clattered down the wood dock.

Kelsie looked nervously from the mare to the heaving deck of the *Suzanne*. The boat tossed at her mooring. Her wood hull was painted a brilliant turquoise and white. You couldn't see the dents Zeke had made with his hooves, but Kelsie knew Gabe had sanded and painted for hours to repair her. What if Diamond kicked his boat to pieces?

Gabe came out of the cabin at the front and squinted at Diamond. "She looks ready to race." Every inch of Diamond's body quivered with pent-up energy. Her high arched neck, sloping shoulders and long, straight legs were built for running. She was hot-blooded, full of energy and exuberance. The wind, wild water and tossing boat all told her to run as fast from this place as she could go.

"We could hobble her . . . once we got her on the deck," Kelsie suggested.

Gabe shook his head. "What would happen if we did that—tied her legs together—and she went overboard?"

"She couldn't swim," gulped Kelsie. "She'd sink like a stone."

As Gabe leaped from the *Suzanne* to the dock, Diamond reared and clawed the air with her front hooves. Gabe jumped back. "Have you considered tranquilizing her?"

"Drugs? We can't." Kelsie bit her lip. "It wouldn't be good for the foal."

Gabe's face fell. "Of course, you're right. I was crazy to offer to take her on the *Suzanne* last night. She must be an enchantress disguised as a horse, putting a spell on me with those big, dark eyes." He grinned. "Or maybe it's you who did the enchanting, Kelsie MacKay."

"Don't joke," Kelsie begged. She could tell that Gabe was on the point of changing his mind about taking Diamond to the island. As for the mare, she had decided this was a dangerous situation. She backed away from the boat, tossing her head in alarm.

"Pull the boat as close to the dock as you can," Kelsie said. "Don't let Diamond see any space between the hull and the dock. Then go in the cabin and wait while I get her on board."

While Gabe snubbed the ropes up tight, Kelsie stood close to Diamond's head, speaking directly to her. "Please trust me. Nothing bad is going to happen if you get on this boat. I'll be right here with you."

Gabe had disappeared into the cabin. Kelsie could see him fiddling with the engine controls. She got a firm grip on Diamond's rope, took a deep breath and led her over the low side of the *Suzanne*'s back deck. Diamond quivered down her whole length, but didn't kick. "There," Kelsie said, letting out her breath. "That wasn't so bad."

"Okay, Gabe," she called to him through the cabin window. "Start her up."

Gabe went forward to undo the bow rope, then hustled back and unknotted the stern rope, leaving it looped around the cleat. "Here!" He tossed her the end of the rope. "Play this out as we swing away from the dock, then let her go once we're clear. It's tricky getting underway in this wind."

Kelsie grabbed the stern rope in one hand. She was still gripping Diamond's lead in the other. "Tricky is right!" she muttered.

"Come on, girl," she said soothingly. "Just stand still while Gabe gets the engine going."

The wind tossed the *Suzanne* up and down. The diesel engine thudded into life, horribly loud. Kelsie could feel its vibration through the planks of the deck. Diamond let out a whinny of fear. "Trust me, trust me," Kelsie pleaded, as Gabe eased the boat out from the dock and she let the rope slide through her hand. If Diamond decided to jump she could be crushed between the hull and the solid timbers of the dock.

Chug, boom, chug, boom—the diesel growled its way into the waves. Spray shot over the bow, wetting Kelsie and her mare. But Kelsie didn't care. They were on their way to Saddle Island at last.

@ @ @

Andy paced the dock in front of his Aunt Maggie's house. It was too rough to take out the skiff—he knew that. But he'd watched Jen in her kayak and then Gabe and Kelsie in the *Suzanne* head out for Saddle Island and he had a sick feeling of being left behind. Dad had made him promise to stay close by the house in case Aunt Maggie needed him.

And where was his dad? Off somewhere, supposedly looking for work. Andy stomped down the dock. Dad had always said he had no time to spend with him because he had to go to work. Now he had no job and he still had no time to go fishing, or play ball, or just hang out. He never cared about me, Andy thought. The job was just an excuse.

"Andy?" His father's voice made him swing around.

Speak of the devil, he thought, expecting a rebuke— something like, "Why aren't you watching your aunt?" As if watching Aunt Maggie sleep would do any good. If she was going to die, like Mom, then she'd die, and nothing he could do would help.

But his father was shielding his eyes with his hand and looking out over the stormy water. "Any sign of your sister and Gabe?" he asked.

"Saw them leave," Andy mumbled, "with that horse."

"I'm glad she's gone." His father sighed. "Things will be a lot better now that hopped-up mare is out of here."

"All the horses will have to come back when it gets cold," Andy pointed out.

"Maybe," his father said. "We'll cross that bridge when we come to it. Right now, we'll have some peace and quiet." He paused. "How's school?"

This was such a stupid question, when Kelsie and Jen and Gabe were out there battling that windy ocean, that Andy couldn't think of an answer except, "Okay."

"Don't get too settled. We might have to leave if I don't find a job," his father went on.

"You could go and we could stay with Aunt Maggie again." Andy kept staring out to sea.

"Sure . . . if . . ." His father paused, then changed the subject. "Jen seems like a nice girl," he said. "What's her mother, Chrissy, like?"

"Nice. I don't know," Andy said, squirming. He didn't want to talk about Jen, or her mother. If the guys at school knew, if he ever even whispered a word about how he and Jen had kissed in that dark tunnel in the summer, about how he felt about her, they'd never quit teasing him. All he could do was not even speak to Jen, and stay as far away from her as possible.

"I was thinking of asking Chrissy out—on a date," his father said.

"NO! Don't do that," Andy shouted. He raced away from his dad, down the dock and into the skiff rocking beside the float. He gripped the motor's starter cord.

"Don't take that boat out. It's too windy," his father yelled after him.

ⓔⓔⓔ

Out on Saddle Island, Jen watched anxiously for any sign of Gabe's fishing boat. The weather was bad. Coming across in her kayak she'd fought the wind to Teapot Island. Gabe might have a hard time swinging into the channel with that wind. And he'll have to come soon, Jen thought, or the causeway rocks will rip the bottom out of the *Suzanne*.

"What do you think, boy?" she asked Caspar. She had ridden the white horse down to the landing at Kelsie's suggestion. The two horses were friends, and Caspar would help make Diamond eager to leave the boat and jump ashore.

She'd left Midnight, Sailor and Zeke behind at the farm. It would be interesting to see how the small band of horses accepted a newcomer—if Diamond made it. Why weren't they in sight?

Caspar snorted and pawed the ground. He'd been acting weird since they got here—did he know Kelsie and Diamond were coming? Or was it something else? Again, Jen had the feeling of being watched. Maybe Caspar felt it, too. His hearing and sense of smell were much better than hers and he could see almost a complete circle around him.

He let out a loud whinny, and at the same time, Jen saw something move out of the corner of her eye. "What was that?" she asked Caspar. "Is there another animal on the island?" There were plenty of deer on these islands but she'd never seen any on Saddle. Maybe a moose had swum out from the mainland. Horses hated moose, for some reason.

Or, Jen wondered, could it possibly be the paddler she'd seen yesterday? If so, why would he be on land, and why would he hide? She heard the unmistakable growl of a big diesel engine, and Gabe's turquoise bow came into view around the dome of Teapot Island.

Jen forgot the paddler. She fixed her gaze on the back deck of the *Suzanne*. What was happening on that boat?

@ @ @

Almost there! Kelsie's arms ached from holding Diamond so tightly. She could see Caspar, a bright white shape against the gray rocks on the island just ahead. "Look," she told Diamond. "You've got a buddy waiting for you."

Maybe Diamond recognized Caspar. Maybe Kelsie relaxed just enough to let the mare feel the possibility of freedom. Whatever the reason, Diamond suddenly yanked the rope out of her grip. She stood, free on the heaving deck for a frightening second, while Kelsie tried to grab the lead rope again.

At that moment a wave lifted the bow of the boat. Diamond scrambled for her balance on the slippery deck and went over the side, into the sea.

It was a terrible, twisting fall, and Diamond disappeared under the surface of the waves.

Kelsie screamed, "Gabe, stop!" but he had already put the engine into reverse.

Kelsie ran to the stern. She saw Diamond's chestnut head break the waves, then another wave swept over the mare. Confused and frantic, she was swimming in a circle, fighting for breath.

There was no way Kelsie could reach her, or help.

10

Don't Drown! @

The wind blew a shout from the shore. Kelsie saw Jen jump up and down and wave her arms. Then she realized why. Caspar had leaped into the water at the landing and was swimming out to Diamond. The wind was against him. One after another, the waves broke over his white head. He appeared, then went under, then appeared again.

"Come on, Caspar!" Kelsie yelled. By now the engine was on idle, and the waves were tossing the *Suzanne* like a toy boat. She knew that soon Gabe would have to leave the swimming horses behind. His boat was in danger of striking the rocks as the tide fell.

Diamond's attempts to stay afloat were getting more feeble. Kelsie could tell the mare was giving up. "Come on, Caspar!" she shouted again.

He reached the side of the boat, threw her a look, but kept swimming toward Diamond. Kelsie saw him nip at her flank as if to say, "Let's go—this way." Then the white horse drove the chestnut mare ahead of him, never letting her stray from a straight path to the shore.

"Look at that!" Gabe shouted over the growl of the engine. "He's herding her to the island!"

Kelsie hugged herself, soaked to the skin with spray. If only the mare's strength would hold. It was a hard swim, even for a horse that loved the water, and Diamond hated it. Kelsie remembered how she had halted at the beach in her wild runaway dash two days ago, as though the ocean was more terrifying than anything she faced on land.

Suddenly, the *Suzanne*'s engine exploded into full throttle. Gabe swung the wheel hard to the right. The fishing boat gave a great lurch. Kelsie gasped as the pointed top of a black rock grazed the boat's bow.

"Can't go any closer!" Gabe shouted from the cabin. "I'll have to turn around and head away from the rocks."

Kelsie nodded. Gabe had no choice. Each time a wave sucked back, it revealed the jagged teeth of the old causeway. As the *Suzanne* swung around, Kelsie ran to the stern. She could see Caspar's white head—but where was Diamond? There! Her chestnut head surfaced, but she was exhausted. The shore was too far—she wasn't going to make it.

Kelsie fell to her knees on the *Suzanne*'s deck. Aunt Maggie had been right. It was reckless and dangerous to try to keep horses on an island. "If Diamond drowns," Kelsie howled to the wind, "I'll never forgive myself."

@ @ @

Alone on the shore of Saddle Island, Jen kept Caspar's white head in view as long as she could. Then she flung herself at her kayak, wriggled into her life jacket, seized the paddle in one hand and the kayak in the other and half dove, half launched the *Seahorse* into the water. The sheltered landing protected her for a few strokes, but once into the channel she had to use her entire body to keep the kayak from swinging out of control.

She leaned forward, throwing every scrap of energy into her stroke. Left, right, left, right. Low in the water, the *Seahorse* sliced through the waves. In seconds, Jen was drenched. A spray skirt would have kept her dry, but she hadn't taken the time to pull it on.

To her surprise, she wasn't alone. From another notch in Saddle Island's western shore, the camouflage-colored kayak sped ahead of her. She saw it reach the swimming horses first, saw a rope swung expertly through the air. It dropped over Diamond's head as if the wind was not blowing, as if thrown from the back of a horse, not the cockpit of a kayak.

Jen was so astonished, for a second she forgot to paddle. It was the mystery paddler, trying to save Diamond. The tug of his rope around the mare's neck was keeping her head above the beating of the waves. They were making their way toward the shore.

Jen turned and waved to Gabe's boat. Gabe was trying to head it away from the jagged rocks.

Jen paddled after the horses and the second kayak. She saw Diamond stumble in the shallows, lose her footing on the slippery, seaweed-covered boulders. Caspar was at her side, urging her upward. The kayaker was speeding away toward the north.

"Wait!" Jen called. "Stop! Come back!" But he was gone. He surfed between two rocks as a large wave surged in and then out, and disappeared. There was no more time to wonder where he'd gone. Jen paddled furiously to the shore, clambered out of her kayak and dragged it up the rocks. Then she ran to help Diamond and Caspar to the shore.

Diamond was almost too weak to pull herself out of the water. Her slender legs weren't built for clambering over wet rocks with the waves beating in on her. Jen waded out into the foam and froth, searching for the end of the rope that was still around her neck.

There—she had it. "Come on, girl, you can make it. It's just a few steps farther!" Jen had to roar over the wind. Caspar was doing his best, whinnying encouragement at Diamond's side.

At last the mare stood on solid ground above the heaving surf. Her proud head drooped and her whole body shuddered. The wind had a new, higher howl, and the trees on the island were bent almost flat. The seabirds had gone to hide, and the island seemed like a scrap of land beaten and left alone in the middle of a hostile sea.

"Let's get you to the barn," Jen urged. She slipped the rope off Diamond, sure the mare would follow her and Caspar down the trail to the farm. But where had the paddler gone, she wondered. And how had he shown up at exactly the right time to throw the rope that saved Diamond? It was almost as though he'd been watching everything that happened.

☙ ☙ ☙

Kelsie stood in the shelter of the *Suzanne*'s cabin, watching the high shape of Saddle Island disappear through the cabin window.

"Any idea who that was in the second kayak?" Gabe stood beside her, his hand on the wheel. They had cleared the causeway rocks and he steered for shore.

Kelsie shook her head numbly. "He seemed to come out of nowhere, but I'm glad he did. I hope Diamond is all right." She pulled back her wind-blown curls. "I wish I were there on the island to help Jen with her. We won't be able to get back in the skiff till this wind dies. And who knows when that will be?"

11

Cold Night ඔ

It was going to be a cold night on Saddle Island. Once Jen had Diamond rubbed down and blanketed in the barn, she looked around and realized the sun would soon set. She had no food or blankets for herself and it was still too windy to paddle back to the mainland. There was one good thing—Kelsie and Gabriel would report she was safe on the island. Her mom wouldn't worry—not too much, anyway.

Jen rubbed Diamond's sensitive ears. "You are a champion," she whispered, "to come through that and be so calm." Diamond responded with a gentle nudge to Jen's shoulder. Her beautiful brown eyes had lost their panicked rim of white and she seemed content to stand in the old stone barn next to Caspar.

But every few minutes another shudder shook the mare's body. Jen was worried about her foal. She knew thoroughbreds weren't like the sturdy Canadian mare, Midnight, or Sailor, the Newfoundland pony, or even Caspar. They were built to take rough weather. Diamond was fine-boned, thin-skinned and delicate.

Jen brought all the horses in. Their body heat would warm the barn. She was starting to shiver, too. She wished she had dry clothes to change into, and a hot drink.

Anything would be better than standing here wet and freezing.

Fire—she needed a fire. She could heat water from the spring. There were matches and candles in the tack box, and an old aluminum pot they had scrounged from Aunt Maggie's kitchen to use for berry picking.

Thinking of berries gave her an idea. Rose hips. The rose bushes that used to grow around the old Ridout Farm had blossomed like mad that summer. The seed pods of the roses were red and plump. They were sour and bitter, but good for the horses because they were loaded with vitamin C.

"Might be okay if I boiled them," Jen murmured to herself. "A lot better than if I just drink plain hot water."

She went shivering out into the night. The wind whined through the tops of the spruce trees, and the sun was hidden behind banks of clouds. It would soon be going down.

Jen knew the horses would have eaten all the rose hips inside the fence. She ducked under the wire, avoiding a shock, and worked her way into the tangle of rose bushes.

There! She had found a branch loaded with fat red rose hips. Jen twisted one off and put it in her mouth. It tasted sour and mushy, and was full of hard seeds. She spat it out. Maybe they would taste better boiled. Jen picked more, plunking them into her pot. When she had enough she headed for the spring to fill the pot with water. Near the spring was an old rock wall. Jen pulled some of the rocks down into a rough circle to make a fire pit. Now, kindling, and firewood. There were plenty of small dead spruce boughs on every tree and they'd burn fast and hard. Behind the barn there was a pile of old roof beams, already charred from an ancient fire.

Jen hurried to get the wood.

Near the barn, she stopped. Someone else was moving toward the barn door. She had forgotten all about the paddler in her struggle to get Diamond warm and dry. She saw a tall figure pause before opening the door and put his ear to the wood as if listening for something.

Jen was about to rush forward but there was something about the way the man was acting that made her wary. "I'm here," she said, stepping forward.

The man twisted to face her. "Where is the mare?" she heard him say. His voice was low and he spoke with an accent.

"She's in the barn," Jen told him. "Who are you?" The man was powerfully built. He was wearing a short jacket and jeans.

He didn't answer. Instead, he asked, "Is she all right?"

"Yes. Would you like to see her?" It was natural for him to take an interest, Jen thought, having swung that rope so expertly over Diamond's neck.

"I would like to do that." The man followed Jen back to the barn and waited while she opened the door.

"She's here," Jen said, "in the first stall." The other horses stamped their feet and nickered a welcome to Jen.

It was already dark inside the barn. The man pulled a flashlight from his jacket pocket and shone it around the interior. "These are all the horses you have rescued, yes?" he asked.

How does he know that, Jen wondered. "That's right," she said, trying to keep the surprise out of her voice.

The man shone his light on Diamond. Her shiny chestnut hide glowed in its beam. She had stopped shivering.

"You dried her off good." He stepped into the stall, ran his hand along Diamond's back. "She looks okay."

He sounds as if this is his horse, Jen thought. And as if he isn't surprised she's here. It doesn't make sense. "You saved her, with your rope," she said. "Where did you learn to throw a lasso like that?"

"I work with horses in Corsica," the man said, running his hand down Diamond's legs to check for soundness. He straightened up and looked at Jen. "I bet you didn't know there were cowboys in Corsica."

"I-I'm not really sure where Corsica is," stammered Jen. There were more puzzles to this man than squares on a Sudoku game.

"It's an island." The man stepped out of the stall. "Like this one, but much bigger. It's near Italy."

"In Europe?" Jen gulped. "That's a long way away."

The man gave a quick nod, then asked, "What is in the pot?"

"Oh!" Jen said. "Rose hips—you know, the seeds from roses. I was going to try to make tea with them."

"You have fire?" The man stepped closer.

"No, but I can make one . . ." Jen started to say.

"I have fire, tea, food. You look very cold. You come with me and get warm."

Jen knew she shouldn't go anywhere with this strange man. She had no idea who he was or what he was doing on the island. She was almost sure he was the one who'd been watching her. But he had also saved Diamond.

She was very cold, and very hungry. The thought of food and a warm fire was too much. "Is it far?" she asked. "Because I should stay near the horses."

"Of course. Not far," the man said. "My name is Victor." He held out a rough hand.

"Mine is Jen." Jen shook it.

"Fine. Let's go."

இ இ இ

"You've got to let us go back to the island, Dad." Kelsie looked from Andy and her father to Chrissy. All four of them stood on her Aunt Maggie's dock. "We can't leave Jen out there by herself all night, and it will soon be too dark to paddle back by herself, won't it, Mrs. Morrisey?"

Kelsie was deliberately not mentioning the strange paddler they'd seen. She didn't want to alarm her dad and Jen's mom. The paddler had helped Diamond—he was probably just a tripper, not a psychotic killer loose on the island.

"Jen's wet, and cold, and there's nothing out there to eat," Kelsie went on. "Please, say yes, before it gets too dark for us to go."

"This is ridiculous." Doug strode up and down the dock. "I feel like I'm being blackmailed into letting you do something dangerous. What about the wind?"

"It's dying down." Kelsie pointed to the water in the cove, which up until a few minutes before had been tossing with whitecaps. "The blow is almost over."

"She's right," Chrissy put in. "I heard the forecast. Light winds tonight."

"And tomorrow's Saturday, so we don't have to go to school. Andy is a really good, safe driver in the skiff." Kelsie shot a look at her younger brother. His face was an unreadable mix of emotions.

Doug looked out at the near shore of Fox Island. In flat light after the storm it seemed close.

"And we don't go out in the open ocean, Dad," Kelsie promised. "We island-hop—they're close together. It's no big deal, honestly. I don't want Jen to get hypothermia."

"What do you think?" Doug turned to Chrissy.

"I think . . . maybe . . . if they promise to be careful . . ." Chrissy looked worried and her large eyes, so much like Jen's, were very blue.

"All right?" Kelsie pressured her dad. "Let me go and grab sleeping bags and food while you talk it over. Then, if you decide it's okay, we'll be ready."

"I'd go with them if it weren't for Aunt Maggie," Doug

said, still striding up and down the dock.

"I understand," Chrissy murmured. "The kids are pretty responsible."

"What do you think, skipper?" Doug turned to Andy. "You've been awful quiet."

Andy's face was red. The thought of Jen, cold and alone on Saddle Island, was terrible. The thought of how the guys would tease him if they knew he'd spent a night with her on the island was terrible. It was a choice between two terrible things. "We should go before dark," he finally mumbled. "Like now."

12

Signals ℗

Ten minutes later, Doug and Chrissy stood side by side on Aunt Maggie's dock. They watched the small green skiff disappearing around the end of Fox Island. "I hope the kids will be okay, staying overnight," Chrissy murmured.

"I probably shouldn't have let them go," said Doug, "but Kelsie's so headstrong. She's used to being in charge, making decisions. Since her mother died, I haven't reined her in the way I should have. It's hard when you're a single parent."

"I know," Chrissy said. "I was sorry to hear about your wife."

"Yeah," said Doug. "Two years ago. The kids took it rough. Especially Andy."

Chrissy didn't say anything for a minute. Then she said: "They're nice kids. My Jen, too. But they grow up fast."

"You're right," said Doug. "That's why I didn't want Kelsie living in the mining camp where I was working. Girls grow up too fast in some of those places." The skiff had disappeared around the point and now its wake sloshed up against the dock timbers. "I'd better get back to Aunt Maggie," he told Chrissy.

They walked slowly up the dock together.

"If you ever need help with your aunt, let me know," said Chrissy.

"Thanks, but Kelsie's a pretty good nurse, when she puts her mind to it. It's this horse business!" Doug waved his arms in frustration. He was thinking that he'd love to take Chrissy up on her offer—he might need help tonight.

But Andy would not like him taking that step.

As Chrissy watched him disappear into the blue house she thought that Douglas had seemed almost human, back there. Why had he shut down when she offered to help? Poor Kelsie, she thought. She has a lot of responsibility for a thirteen-year-old.

ⓠ ⓠ ⓠ

Dusk fell around the small motorboat as it lumbered over the swells left from the wind. Kelsie kept a careful eye out for rocks. The tide was falling dangerously low. "Slow down, Andy," she called to her brother.

"It's hard to control her if I go too slow," Andy roared back, but he twisted the throttle lever to a lower speed.

Kelsie swung her flashlight beam left and right in front of the skiff's bow, hoping to see the outline of a rock before they hit it. She watched for swirling water, the eddies that waves made around the largest rocks. There—right ahead!

"More to the left!" she shouted and felt the skiff lurch

away from the rock. "Slow down, Andy. That one almost got us." The jagged black boulder seemed to sweep down the skiff's side.

"I can't go much slower!" Andy yelled back. "The waves toss us around like wood chips at these revs."

They were silent for a moment. The waves heaved the skiff up and down like a rocking horse. Kelsie couldn't see Andy's face in the fading light. "Why didn't you want to come to the island tonight?" she asked him.

"I don't know—doesn't matter," he mumbled.

"And why are you acting like Jen isn't your friend since we started school?" Kelsie demanded.

"None of your business," Andy growled.

"It is my business because Jen is my friend and you're hurting her feelings," Kelsie insisted. "She thinks you don't like her anymore."

"I came, didn't I?" Andy exploded, as if the words burst out of him like a cork from a bottle. "I like Jen. Just don't talk about her like she's my girlfriend."

" 'Cause it isn't cool to like a girl now that you're in grade seven?"

Andy groaned. "I don't want to talk about it, Kel."

"All right." Kelsie sighed. "The important thing is to get to the island. It's cold out here—Jen must be freezing."

@ @ @

Jen followed the tall man named Victor up the trail along Saddle Island's west side. It was an old road, overgrown with trees and brush. Jen knew this route well. It was the way to her high rock perch at the tip of the island—the Saddlehorn.

That can't be where we're going, she thought. Nobody knows about the trail to the top except me and Kelsie and Andy.

Sure enough, before they reached the Saddlehorn cutoff, Victor swung off to the right. We must be heading for the northeast corner of Saddle Island, Jen realized, where the sea pounds in on bare rocks, and almost nothing grows. It's the rockiest and roughest shore on the entire island—exposed to the open ocean. What a weird place to camp!

It was getting dark and Victor switched on his flashlight. Even though the wind was dying, huge waves were swamping the shore when they reached the bare rocks, sending plumes of spray high in the air. They were phosphorescent in the darkness, beautiful and powerful.

Victor's fire was a small glow in the shelter between two slabs of rock.

His camouflaged kayak, a small domed tent and some cooking gear near the fire made up his camp. He handed her his flashlight and put another stick of driftwood on the coals.

As it flared up, Jen saw Victor's face more clearly. He had large, chiseled features, a prominent nose and jutting brows. He was not young, and despite the way he'd rescued Diamond, there was something about the way he clenched his jaw that made Jen shiver. What had she done, following this man here? I should have got in my kayak and paddled home, she thought.

He turned to her. "Want some coffee?" he asked in his low, accented voice.

"Uh. I . . . s-sure," she managed to stammer. She didn't like the taste of coffee, but it would be hot.

"Okay, sit here." He pointed at a sloping ledge of rock, then reached into the pocket of his vest. "Here. Eat some of this."

It was a chocolate bar. Jen broke off a bite and tried to hand it back. But Victor had turned his back to her, staring out to sea. Jen could see another light out on the water. What was that?

Victor swung his powerful flashlight up and blinked it on and off three times. Some kind of signal, Jen thought. That must be why he's camped here—he needs to be in touch with the boat.

Suddenly, the chocolate stuck in her throat. Victor wasn't just a sea kayaker—he was a smuggler. He was signaling to the ship offshore that was going to land its illegal cargo right here.

But if that was true, why had he brought her to this place? She would be able to tell . . . Jen almost gagged. She'd be able to tell! That's why he'd brought her. To make sure she kept silent. The tea, the warmth, the chocolate, was just a trick to keep her close. She had to get away!

As if he had read her mind, he shone the flashlight beam in her eyes. "Stay here!" he commanded. "I must climb to the top of the rocks to make a better signal." With strong strides he headed up the smooth rock surface above the fire.

"I should go now," Jen whispered to herself, but her shivering legs would not take her far. Victor would be able to hunt her down easily.

He was scrambling down the rock. "Come," he growled. "Hurry. We must go back to the barn. You first. I shine the light."

He was smart—she had no chance to slip away in the darkness if she was ahead of him. Jen's weary body protested as she got to her feet. She was still cold. "No fire? No tea?" she whined. It wasn't hard to pretend this was the worst of her worries.

"Later. We get later. Now we have to go." Victor grabbed Jen's arm and thrust her in front of him. "Run! It will warm you up."

Why are we going back to the barn, she wondered as she stumbled along the dark trail.

13

Meeting at the Barn ✆

Gabriel inspected the hull of his boat, looking for hoof marks on the combing around the rear deck. Surprisingly, it was unmarked. Diamond, as light and elegant as a fine china horse, had gone over the side into the ocean without leaving any sign she'd ever been a passenger on the *Suzanne*. He'd hated to turn back and leave without making sure she and Jen were okay, but getting hung up on one of the causeway rocks—that would cause serious damage to his boat!

Gabe looked out at the sea and the darkening sky. The wind had died to a stiff breeze. He checked his watch. After eight-thirty—the tide would be rising now.

Footsteps running down the wood dock made him turn. Kelsie?

No, it was Steffi and her friends. Like a flock of giddy seagulls, Gabe thought.

"What are you doing?" Steffi asked, her blonde head cocked to one side.

"Not much," he answered. "I just came back from ferrying Kelsie's new mare over to Saddle Island. We had a tough time with the wind and the horse went overboard."

"Exciting." Steffi sounded bored. "What are you gonna do now? Want to come up to the Clam Shack with us?"

"I don't know," Gabe said slowly. "I guess not. I should go see Kelsie and her brother. Offer to take them back to the island later when the tide's higher—around ten." He was thinking out loud, not looking at Steffi's face or he would have seen her furious scowl. "Another time, Steff. See you, girls."

He walked away up the dock with his long stride.

"Oh!" Steffi stamped her foot. "You've had it, Gabriel Peters."

"What are you going to do?" one of her friends huddled close to ask.

"Don't know. But something. I'm not having him spend the night with those brats on Saddle Island, I can tell you that!"

☙ ☙ ☙

Meanwhile, on the island, Jen and Victor had reached the old barn. The whinnying of five horses greeted them. Jen opened the door to the warm breath and stampings of five sets of hooves on the wood floor.

Jen went from one to the other, stroking muzzles, straightening forelocks, rubbing cheeks. Caspar blew softly in her ear as if glad to see her back. "Thanks for taking care of everything," she whispered to him. Diamond was quiet and not shaking with cold. She seemed content munching hay from a net.

Victor's voice made her jump. "Get the mare." He shone his light on Jen and the racehorse.

"Diamond? What for?"

"She is going on a trip."

What was he talking about, Jen wondered. "Where?" she asked.

Victor didn't answer. He took a step toward Diamond's stall and she threw up her head in warning. "She's tired," Jen said. "She needs to rest."

"Not tonight," Victor growled. "Tonight she has to travel. Far from here. Get her bridle."

Jen felt a chill of fear run down her arm as she reached for Diamond's bridle, hung on a nail by the stall. As if she had transmitted her fear to the horse, Diamond let out a shrill whinny.

Jen was thinking furiously. Drug smuggling, and a horse? How did any of this make sense?

"Is that why you rescued her with your rope?" she asked.

"Of course." Victor's nod was brief, proud. "It is my job to look after her."

"So you've been watching, and waiting, and hanging around the island until Diamond got here . . ." Jen was shaking from head to foot. Her wet clothes felt heavy on her body. She remembered all those times she had felt someone watching her.

"Sure," Victor nodded again. "And tonight I signal the

boat that she is here. They tell me they are ready. We have to go now."

"But why a horse?"

"Why not?" Victor scowled. "This is none of your business."

Just then they heard voices outside the barn. Jen sucked in a deep breath of relief. "My friends are here," she said bravely. "Kelsie rescued Diamond—it's her business what happens to this mare."

The scowl on Victor's face deepened. He jerked the bridle from Jen's hand. "Go!" he snapped. "Tell them to stay away."

It was too late. Kelsie and Andy came through the barn door. Andy had a backpack slung over his shoulder and a flashlight in his hand. "Hi, Jen. We brought you . . ." He stopped when he saw Victor. "Wh-who?" he stuttered.

"You're the guy who saved Diamond, aren't you?" Kelsie stepped forward. "The man in the kayak."

"No time to talk," Victor said. "I must take the mare to the ship." He bridled Diamond with a practiced hand. "You kids must stay here."

"Wait a minute," Kelsie said, crossing to Diamond's stall. "Where are you taking my horse?"

Jen tried to flash her a warning signal but Kelsie was too alarmed to catch it.

"She is not your horse. Anyway, you almost kill her bringing her here on that boat. If it not be for me she drowned." Victor seized Diamond's reins and led her out of her stall, holding her close to his body so she couldn't kick or lash out.

As he passed Kelsie she saw something on the sleeve of his jacket that made the hairs on the back of her neck prickle. It was a smear of scarlet paint—the same blood red as the paint on the truck door Caspar had backed into. Her mind spun. That was the day Diamond came. The rescue society truck! "Are you with the Racehorse Rescue Society?" she gasped.

Victor paused. His bushy eyebrows rose and fell. "Sure," he said finally. "So this is my mare. We take her to a better place." He looked around the barn. "This island is no good."

"What do you mean you're taking her? How? Where?" Kelsie insisted.

"There's a ship off the northeast shore," Jen shot in. "It came to get her."

"That is right." Victor led Diamond toward the door. "The ship wait for us now. Don't worry. This horse will have a very good life—she and her foal will live in a barn like a palace with other fine horses—not like these nags." He gave Midnight, Zeke, Sailor and Caspar a contemptuous nod.

Kelsie and Jen shared a glance. Dr. Bricknell had been right about the foal!

"Don't worry," Victor repeated, "but don't come near the shore. My friends on the ship do not like kids." He turned back, his forehead set in a menacing frown. "I mean it. Stay away from the shore."

They followed him and Diamond to the barn door. "Stay

here!" Victor ordered once more. He climbed on Diamond's bare back. She skittered and shied, but he handled her like an expert jockey and soon had her headed down the trail at a gallop.

His bobbing light disappeared. Diamond's hoof beats faded in the distance. The three friends stood in the barn doorway, listening.

Behind them, Caspar whickered nervously.

"He doesn't like this," said Kelsie. "Neither do I."

"But if the guy's from the rescue society what can you do?" Andy shrugged.

"Why would they bring Diamond all the way to Dark Cove and then ship her away in the dead of night?" Kelsie demanded.

"It's only nine o'clock," said Jen. She peered at her watch by the flashlight's dim glow. "It just feels like the middle of the night. Maybe they had to wait for the tide to rise to bring their boat in . . ."

"And another thing," Kelsie said. "Andy, do you remember that paint smear on Caspar's rear from the rescue truck?"

Andy nodded. "Yeah . . . so?"

"So, Victor has a red smear just like it on his jacket. He must have come to Dark Cove with Diamond and jumped out of the truck before I met it. But why was the lettering on the truck wet? I'll bet I know why—they painted an ordinary pickup so they'd look like a rescue society. That woman . . ." Kelsie paused and gulped, "she didn't seem like the real thing and neither does Victor. They lied about everything."

Andy looked thoughtful. "Maybe you're right. If Diamond was just a broken-down racehorse on her way to the dog food factory, why did they go to all this trouble? Why is she worth so much to them? I mean, a fake truck, and a ship . . ." He waved his arms in the air.

Jen said, "I have a horrible idea. I thought Victor was signaling a drug smuggler's ship from the shore. Maybe they hid drugs inside Diamond's body."

"That's too awful!" exclaimed Kelsie. "But Victor said she and her foal would have a good life wherever they're going. Maybe Diamond isn't a broken-down has-been. Maybe she's a valuable racehorse and she's been stolen. Whatever the truth is, we have to get her away from these guys. Let's go!"

"Are you out of your mind?" Andy grabbed her arm. "You just said they're thieves, or international drug smugglers. And you heard what Victor said—we should stay away. Far, far away. It's just a horse, Kel."

Kelsie and Jen both turned and gave him a look.

"Okay, little brother," Kelsie said. "You go back to the landing, get your skiff and go for help. That makes sense. Jen and I will take the horses and go save Diamond, if we can."

Andy's shoulders sagged. "If you're going to do something that dumb, I'm coming, too." He glanced at Jen. "I'm not letting you race off to the rescue by yourselves."

"We sh-should hurry," Jen said. She was starting to shiver uncontrollably.

"Okay, but first," Andy said to her shyly, "you should change your wet clothes." He swung the backpack off his shoulder and zipped it open. "You're freezing. We brought dry clothes for you and some hot chocolate."

Jen took the insulated flask from his hand and unscrewed the lid. The warm sweet liquid poured down her throat, warming her from the inside. She smiled. "Thanks, Andy."

14

Gabe Tries to Help ✆

Dressed in warm clothes and with hot, sweet chocolate inside, Jen felt like a new person, ready for anything. What had Andy called it—a race to the rescue? That's what they had to do. Rescue Diamond!

Kelsie was busily bridling Caspar for herself, Zeke for Jen and Sailor for Andy.

"This takes time but we can go much faster with the horses," she panted, leading Sailor out of his stall and handing his reins to Andy. "Do you need a saddle? I don't want you falling off."

"Don't worry," said Andy, ruffling Sailor's fuzzy forelock. "This guy's like a circus pony. He's fun to ride bareback, aren't you, buddy?"

Jen grinned at him, and took another swallow from the flask. Andy had only learned to ride a few weeks ago, but Sailor tried to make it easy for him. The little Newfoundland pony had been a school horse for the youngest riders. He knew how to go gently and with almost no direction. But Jen would never say that to Andy!

"Ready, Jen?" Kelsie asked as she led Caspar out of the barn. "Zeke's all set."

Jen went to get the lean brown horse from his stall. She knew he'd be nervous, riding at night on a strange trail to the shore. And who knew what they'd meet up with once they got there? "Don't worry," Jen soothed him as she led him out to the others. "You're just going on a nice ride with friends."

She hoped she was right.

☙ ☙ ☙

At around nine-thirty, Gabriel knocked at the door of Aunt Maggie's blue house. "I'm looking for Kelsie," he told Doug when he opened the door. "I guess she told you about almost getting the *Suzanne* stuck on the rocks. The tide's higher now and I could take Kelsie over to the island . . . if she likes . . . and it's okay with you."

He stopped. Doug was looking him over as if he'd come to take Kelsie out on a date. Gabe could feel his ears getting hot.

"Kelsie's not here," Doug said. "She and Andy took the skiff to the island to meet Jen. They're staying for the night." He gave Gabe another sharp look. "So there's no need for you to take your boat over there."

"No, uh, sure . . ." Gabe stammered. "I just thought to make sure the kids and the horse are all right—that mare had quite a fall."

"They're all right," Doug said firmly. "And it would be my job to worry about them if they weren't."

Gabriel felt a spurt of annoyance. He'd come here to offer help and he was being treated like some kind of threat. "All right," he said. "I'll be seeing you, then."

No use telling Kelsie's dad about all the times he'd got Kelsie out of trouble since she'd arrived in Dark Cove. He'd plucked her off dangerous rocks, picked her up out of ditches, helped transport horses to the island. The kid was a magnet for trouble. It wasn't exactly that she looked for it, but she wasn't afraid of anything, and she acted before she thought—a dangerous combination.

"Why do you worry so much about Kelsie?" he muttered to himself. "It's not like she's your kid sister or anything." He couldn't answer that question. There was just something about Kelsie, with her flying red curls and green eyes and challenging look, that made him want to look after her. "Her dad should worry," he said, under his breath. "That island has a bad history. And who was that paddler we saw?"

ⓔⓔⓔ

"Who was that at the door?" Aunt Maggie called from her sun porch bedroom.

"Gabriel Peters." Doug walked down the hall and leaned against the doorframe. His aunt was sitting straight up in her bed.

"Gabriel!" Aunt Maggie's face brightened. "What did he want?"

"He wanted to go look for Kelsie and Andy in his lobster boat—as if it was any of his business."

Aunt Maggie's gray eyes widened. "Where are Kelsie and Andy?"

Doug gulped. "They're camping on Saddle Island, with Jen," he said. "They wanted to make sure the new mare gets settled in."

"Listen to me." Aunt Maggie's hands gripped her quilt. "If Gabriel thinks he should go and check on those children, then he should go. That young man knows more about this cove and the islands than anyone." She put her hand to her throat. "Don't forget, your parents were shipwrecked off Saddle Island, on the rocks they call the Five Sisters. My sister Elizabeth, your mother . . ."

"I don't forget." Doug held up his hand. "But don't you think . . . don't you worry that Gabe's a little too old to be bothering about Kelsie? She's only thirteen."

"Nonsense!" Aunt Maggie shook her head angrily. "Gabriel's not that kind of boy. Kelsie and Andy are like family to him. I'd trust him with them anywhere. Did you send him away, Douglas?"

"Not really," Doug said. But he knew he had.

ⓐ ⓐ ⓐ

Walking back to his dock, Gabe stared out to sea. He was stinging from the way Kelsie's dad had spoken to him, but still worried. Kelsie had told him she'd seen lights on the far side of the island. Yes! There they were. He could see a flash, just beyond Saddle Island's north end.

Gabe lengthened his stride. It wouldn't hurt to take the

Suzanne out there with her own powerful light—maybe scare off the smugglers, if that's who it was.

@ @ @

On Gabe's dock, Steffi and her friends were bent over a plastic tube and a bucket. They had thrust the other end of the tube into the *Suzanne*'s fuel tank.

"I have to hurry if I'm going to siphon gas out of his boat," Steffi said. "It's almost ten and Gabriel will be leaving."

"You suck on this end," one of Steffi's friends told her. "I've seen my brother do it. When the gas comes in your mouth you put the end down in the pail and spit."

"Ugh!" Steffi tucked her blonde hair into the collar of her shirt.

"You must really want revenge, to do this," one of her friends said.

"I wouldn't do it for anything," agreed another.

At that second the diesel shot up the tube. Steffi swung it over to the pail, spat into the ocean and watched the stream of diesel fuel flow.

"Someone's coming," a third friend hissed.

"It's Gabe," one of the girls whispered. "We'd better get out of here."

The four girls took their bucket and slid away in the darkness.

"Just try to get to Saddle Island now, Gabriel Peters," Steffi said, giggling. "You won't get far."

۞ ۞ ۞

Meanwhile, the vet, Dr. Bricknell, was on the phone in his office.

"I'm sorry we couldn't get back to you until tonight," the man on the other end of the line said. "It's been one of those days."

"But you're sure this is the Thoroughbred Rescue Society?" Dr. Bricknell insisted. "The official, recognized organization that adopts out racehorses?"

"Yes, why?"

Dr. Bricknell told his story. "I believe the mare is in foal," he explained. "They dropped her off with a young client of mine without telling her. No paperwork whatsoever. Would your organization ever do that?"

"Not a chance. Are you sure she's a thoroughbred? Some people . . ."

"She has the tattoo inside her lip," Dr. Bricknell explained.

"Did you record the number?"

"No, I should have, but I didn't think of it until later."

"Well, if you can get that number and call us back, with a full description of the mare, we can trace her on the registry—no problem."

"Thank you, I'll do that tomorrow." The vet hung up the phone. He had no way of knowing that at this moment Diamond was clattering down the rocks of Saddle Island's windy shore.

15

Dark Journeys @

Kelsie galloped Caspar along the trail to the northeast shore. The horses could see in the dark and now the moonlight was bright enough that she could see the way ahead. If only they could reach the shore before Diamond was forced aboard that ship!

Behind she could hear the hoofbeats of Jen on Zeke and Andy on Sailor. They were too far away to call to each other. As she swung Caspar toward the northeast corner of the island, Kelsie wondered at what point they should dismount and lead the horses closer. Everything depended on surprise.

When she could clearly hear the sound of the surf, she slowed to let Jen and Andy catch up. "We should leave the horses," she told Jen. "If Victor hears them, he'll know we're here."

Quickly, they tied Sailor, Zeke and Caspar to the skinny spruces that grew back from the shore. Kelsie whispered in Caspar's ear. "You stay put, and don't get any ideas about untying knots and following us." Just to make sure, she tied

Caspar's rope extra tight. He had been known to free himself and the other horses he was with.

"All right," Kelsie told Jen. "You lead—you know where the campfire is."

They were glad of the moonlight. It lit the tops of the smooth rock ledges, leaving the hollows in blackness. They crept over the top of a ledge and saw below it a flicker of orange. Victor's fire.

Beyond, the sea heaved and rolled, with the moonlight making a bright path across the waves.

"Tide's coming in," Jen said. "The fire was farther from the water when I was here before."

"There's Victor," Kelsie gasped, pointing to a dark figure on the highest outcrop of rock. He flashed a light, and an answering flash came from the ship.

"We're just in time. He's signaling the smugglers to come and get Diamond," Kelsie said with a shiver.

"Can you see her?" hissed Jen.

"No. She must be on the other side of the fire. We'll circle around and see if we can snatch her right out from under Victor's nose while he's concentrating on his signals."

"You two are totally crazy," they heard Andy mutter behind them. "We shouldn't be here."

"Just get ready to run back to the horses," Kelsie told him. "I'll jump on Diamond's back and ride like the wind out of here. We'll meet . . ."

"Not back at the barn," Andy said. "That's the first place they'll look."

"Right, good thinking," Kelsie said, "but where?"

"Why not down at the treasure pit," suggested Jen. "Victor might not know that part of the island."

"Under the big spruce—right!" Kelsie gripped Jen's hand. "Okay. Here goes. Stay close!"

They slithered down the sloping rock-face toward the fire, trying to keep to the shadows.

@ @ @

The *Suzanne* rose and fell helplessly as the swells swept under her deck. Gabriel cursed his stalled engine. What was wrong? A few minutes in the engine compartment under the deck told him the truth. "Out of fuel!" he exclaimed. "How did that happen? I filled up the tank yesterday."

Who would steal diesel out of his tank? Suddenly, Gabe thought of Steffi's angry face. She hadn't wanted him to go so she made sure he'd never reach Saddle Island. He hadn't realized she was capable of such a mean trick. Not only mean, he thought, but dangerous. Steffi should know better!

Gabe let out the anchor to hold the *Suzanne* steady. He should have brought a spare can of diesel, he thought. He might have if he was going to be fishing all day, but this was such a short trip.

From where he sat, he could see the looming shape of Saddle Island's high north end. No sign of a light from a ship. It had either gone, or was behind the island. Gabe paced the heaving deck in frustration. He could radio for help, but the coast guard wouldn't be happy about responding to a stupid call like "out of fuel." Better to wait till morning, and wave down another boat.

☙ ☙ ☙

In Dark Cove, Doug paced the small floor of the parlor in his aunt's house, stopping every once in a while to rub his beard and peer out the window that faced the sea. Aunt Maggie had fallen into a restless sleep, but when she woke up she would ask if Gabriel had gone over to the island to see if the kids were okay. He didn't know what to tell her.

Finally, he grabbed his jacket and headed out the door. He hated to go back to the Peters kid after the way he'd talked to him, but he had to admit he was wrong and needed help.

He walked the curved beach, listening to the rollers pounding in. The waves were still big from the wind earlier in the day. In the fifteen minutes it took to reach Gabe's dock he rehearsed what he'd say: "Sorry, Gabe, I really would appreciate it if you'd just run out to the island and check on Kelsie and Andy."

But when he reached the Peters' dock, Gabe and the *Suzanne* had gone. Four girls sat under the light at the end of the dock. They giggled when they saw him.

"Have you seen Gabriel Peters?" He looked down at them.

A blonde girl stood up and said, "We've seen him, but he's not here."

"Do you know if he went to Saddle Island?" Doug tried to sound casual. "I wondered if he'd gone to look for my kids."

The four girls burst into torrents of laughter. When they could talk, the blonde girl gasped, "No, he didn't go to the island."

"That's for sure," another girl added with a snort. "No way."

Something was going on, but Doug knew they'd never let him in on their secret. "If you see him, tell him Doug was looking for him," he finally said, and that made the girls laugh even harder.

"We won't see him," gasped one. "Not for a long, long time."

Doug walked away from the group of girls and the dock. What now, he wondered. He saw a light in the Morrisey house a little way up the hill. Funny how he remembered that was where the Morriseys had always lived. He even remembered Chrissy as a little girl, shy and quiet. She'd looked a lot like Jen, with soft brown hair and very blue eyes. He found himself climbing up the hill and knocking on her door.

She looked surprised to see him. "Doug! Anything wrong?"

"I don't know," he said, suddenly embarrassed. "But Aunt Maggie seems to be worried about the kids. And I can't find Gabe."

"Come in." Chrissy held the door open for him.

"I shouldn't stay," Doug told Chrissy. "I don't like to leave Aunt Maggie by herself."

"I'll walk back with you," Chrissy said, reaching for her jacket. "You're worrying too much. Our kids can look after themselves for one night."

They headed out along the gravel road that led between the two houses. "How's it working out, being back in Dark Cove?" asked Chrissy.

"Not very well," Doug admitted. "I'm used to working, having a job, being out of the house."

Chrissy nodded in the darkness.

"I know the kids want to stay here," Doug went on, "but I'm not sure I can stick it out. The house is too small for four of us."

Some families had thirteen kids in houses like that, thought Chrissy, but she didn't say anything. It was hard enough to get Doug talking.

She looked out to sea. The moon made a silvery path on the water that led to the islands and beyond. Way out, she saw the lights from a ship flash. "Did you see that?" she asked Doug. "There's some kind of boat out there."

He looked where she pointed, but the light had gone.

16

Smugglers' Game ◎

Trying to hurry but not be heard, Kelsie, Andy and Jen worked their way to the other side of the fire. There was no sign of Diamond.

"Where is she?" Kelsie whispered.

"Listen!" Andy put his fingers to his lips. "Shhh!" They could all hear the sound of an outboard motor approaching the shore.

"That must be a boat they've sent to pick her up," Kelsie said. "They're landing on the other side of this rock outcrop. Come on!"

"But Victor will see you—he'll be looking right down at you," Andy protested.

"He'll be watching the boat. Come on!" Kelsie grabbed her brother's arm. The three of them scurried around the rocks, keeping low. As they rounded the corner, their eyes were momentarily blinded by a searchlight. It came from a small barge the ship had sent, and it was scanning the shore for a good landing spot.

Then, in its bright beam, Kelsie saw a flash of chestnut hide. She gasped, "There's Diamond! That beast Victor has hobbled her front legs so she can't run! Jen—come with me and undo the rope while I get on her back."

"Stop! It's too dangerous," Andy tried to warn them, but it was too late. Jen and Kelsie were already running toward Diamond.

Diamond let out a whinny of greeting. Jen fumbled with the rope around her forelegs. Diamond stamped and struggled to be free. "Hold still, we're here to help you!" Kelsie cried, trying to leap aboard the mare.

At that second she heard a wild shout from Andy. "Get . . . OFF ME!"

She turned to see Victor dragging Andy toward them. Andy squirmed in his grip, but Victor's huge fist was wrapped around his arm like a vice. "What you think you are doing!" he howled at Kelsie and Jen. "Stay away from my horse!"

"Run!" Andy shouted. "He's only got two hands—he can't grab us all!"

"I don't think they will run away and desert you," Victor said. His voice sank to a growl. "You should not have come here."

Kelsie saw him give Andy's arm a nasty twist. A shout of rage rose to her throat. "Let my brother go!"

"No! Now it is too late. The boat is coming." Victor shone his light on the water. They saw a flat barge nosing into the shore. The steel hull slid over the shingle shore with a harsh, scraping sound. The metal doors grated open.

Diamond reared and whinnied in terror.

Two men were striding through the surf and clambering over the rocks toward the fire. Both wore hooded yellow rain slickers. Under the hoods, one face was dark and bearded, the other fair and clean-shaven. They looked eagerly at Diamond.

"There she is, our valuable passenger," the bearded man said. He had a British accent. "Our fortune on four legs."

The other man had zeroed in on Andy and the two girls. "What have you got here?" he shouted. "Victor, explain this, now!"

"They came to the island with the mare." Victor shook Andy like an angry dog. "I tried to lose them . . ."

"Get rid of them," the bearded man ordered, "while we get the horse on board. And hurry—we've waited long enough for you and this animal."

The fair-haired man was trying to untie Diamond. She lashed out, threatening to trample him into the rocks.

"She won't go with you," Kelsie shouted at him. "She's afraid of loud clanging metal things, like starting gates and your barge."

"Take the girl," Victor said. "She handles the mare well."

"Nah, too much trouble. The three of us can handle one horse," said the fair-haired man.

"You don't know this mare. And if you upset her too much, it may injure her foal," Victor insisted.

"He's the horse expert," growled the bearded man, who seemed to be the boss. "Better listen to him and take the girl."

Jen glanced in horror at Andy. Were they really going to take Kelsie on board the barge? And what was Victor going to do with them before he left with the ship? Her heart was beating so hard she thought it would burst out of her chest. Andy was struggling to free himself from Victor's grip and swearing under his breath. Kelsie had her head thrown back and her hair blazed red in the firelight. She looked like nothing could frighten her.

"Make it look like an accident," the fair-haired man was saying to Victor. "We don't want to leave a trail. I'm not having our whole operation fouled up by a bunch of kids."

"I know what to do," growled the bearded man. He strode to the barge and brought back a red plastic gas can. He handed it to Victor and whispered an order in his ear.

"Let's go, you two." Victor seized Jen's arm with his other hand. "We go back to the barn once more. Move!"

They started up the rocks. Behind them, they could hear Kelsie coaxing Diamond toward the barge.

@ @ @

Over in Dark Cove, Aunt Maggie greeted Chrissy and Doug with a smile of delight. "I've been wondering where this nephew of mine had got to," she said. "But I see he's in good hands. Did you find Gabriel? Did he go and look for the children?"

"I'm sure they're fine." Chrissy pulled up a chair beside Aunt Maggie's bed. "Have you been awake and worrying?"

"No." Aunt Maggie brushed back a strand of stray hair

from her forehead. "I've been asleep. Dreaming of the old days and the stories my father told about when he was a boy and his father and uncle were running rum off Saddle Island. My great-aunt used to leave a light in the window if the coast was clear to bring in a load of illegal rum." She smiled. "Lots of smuggling on the islands in those days. It was a dark and dangerous place."

"No wonder you worry about the kids over there at night, then," Chrissy said. She thought of the light she'd seen out at sea and decided it wouldn't be a good idea to mention that! Aunt Maggie's stories had chilled her heart. People said the smuggling still went on, only now it wasn't rum.

"As soon as I can find Gabe, I'll ask him to go out to check on the kids," said Doug. "Our young lobsterman seems to have disappeared."

Aunt Maggie's face brightened. "I'll lay a bet Gabriel's already gone out to Saddle Island to find them."

@ @ @

"Why is Victor taking us back to the barn?" Jen muttered to Andy as they rode side by side down the dark road across the top of the island. She had to lean down to make him hear. Sailor was at least two hands shorter than Caspar.

"Be quiet," Victor called from behind, on Zeke. "Go faster. I must get back to the ship soon." The red gas can sloshed at his side.

Jen clucked to Caspar and the white horse lengthened his stride. They followed the old road west across the island, south toward the landing and then back east on the cutoff trail to the Ridout farm. Victor rode close behind them and she knew he was watching every move they made.

"I told you we shouldn't try to rescue Diamond," Andy mumbled. "It didn't do any good and now we're in real trouble."

"Forget the 'I told you so' speeches," Jen said. "What do you think Victor's going to do to us?" Her heart hadn't stopped thumping since they'd ridden away from the shore.

"The gas can should give you an idea." Andy's voice was grim. "Gasoline plus an old barn equals fire. The smugglers don't want any witnesses."

"You mean set fire to the barn . . . with us inside?" cried Jen. "He couldn't . . ."

"Stop talking. Get those nags to move!" Victor shouted. Riding Zeke bareback was not improving the man's temper. The nervous brown horse hated the smell of the gas can thumping at his side, hated the rider on his back. He fought the bit, tossed his head and balked at Victor's commands.

"Make a break for it, Jen," Andy hissed. "Zeke's giving Victor a hard time and Caspar's pretty fast. Go!"

"And leave you? No." Jen shook her head. "We're in this together." They both knew Zeke could outrun Andy's little pony.

A few minutes later they rode up to the old farm. The stone barn was a black shape against the night sky.

"Quick. Get those horses inside. Lock them in their stalls,"

Victor ordered. His voice was hoarse. "Take this monster with you."

"Zeke's not a monster if you treat him right," Jen said, under her breath. She took Zeke's reins from Victor's hands. "C'mon, boy."

By Victor's bobbing light, she and Andy led Caspar, Zeke and Sailor to their stalls. The man turned his light on Midnight, placidly munching hay in the stall nearest the door.

"I ride this horse back to the shore," he announced. "She is fresh, and seems steady. Get her ready."

Jen went for Midnight's tack. She felt tears close to the surface as she saddled and bridled the sturdy black mare, straightening her curly mane and stroking her warm strong neck. At least Midnight would escape this nightmare.

"Now I tie you," Victor said. He reached in his pocket for a ball of blue nylon cord, the kind they used to tie straw bales.

"Don't tie us up!" Andy cried. "We won't run away."

"I take no chances," grunted Victor. He rested his flashlight on an overturned bucket, then shoved Andy against Caspar's stall. "You foolish boy—why you not stay here when I tell you in the first place?"

He bound Andy's wrists together and tied him to the stall door. "This hold you good," he muttered. He turned to Jen. "And you—here." He motioned Jen against Zeke's stall. "You like this horse? I tie you up near him."

He tied Jen to Zeke's stall with her hands over her head. Helpless, the thin cord cutting their wrists, they watched while Victor unscrewed the top of the gas can.

17

Fire!

"You don't want to do this." Andy tried to keep his voice calm. "If you burn down this barn you'll be a murderer."

"You can't burn the horses alive!" Jen was struggling not to cry. "They haven't done anything."

Victor hesitated, the gas can tipped in his hand, ready to spill on the dry hay. They could already smell the fumes. Zeke stamped in the stall behind them.

"We won't tell anyone about your stupid smuggling scheme," Andy promised. "Why should we? It doesn't matter to us what you do with Diamond."

With a thump, Victor put down the gas can. Gas sloshed out the open top.

"I am horse thief, crooked horse trainer. I fix races, sometimes," he said in his deep voice. "I am not killer of horses. But these men on ship are very bad. If I let you go, they will kill me." He pointed to Jen. "And you I cannot trust to let go. You will come back to shore for your friend. You will tell police."

They could see fear sweep over Victor's face. He shook his head. "I have no choice. My boss gave the order. You should not have interfered."

"Wait!" Jen shouted. "If the men on the ship see a huge fire and smell smoke they'll think the barn is on fire, right?"

Victor stared at her.

"There's a big pile of charred beams behind the barn," Jen rushed on. "If you pour gas on that and light it, it will make lots of smoke and flames."

"That's right," Andy's words stumbled over each other. "Leave us tied. We won't be able to get away. It will be hours before anyone comes to the island looking for us."

"Even then we won't tell. Please," Jen begged. "Set the fire outside and save the horses."

Victor was still staring at them. Then he blinked. "I see a barn fire one time," he said. "It was terrible thing . . . many horses died." He picked up the gas can and screwed the lid on tight. "I am not a killer, but I leave you tied. I lock you in."

He left them in darkness, shutting and bolting the barn door from the outside. They waited while he thumped around to the back of the barn. There was a pause, then an enormous WHOOSH as the gasoline-soaked beams exploded into flame. Over the fire's roar they heard hoofbeats thudding away.

"He's gone." Jen sagged against the cord that held her hands over her head.

"Listen to that fire," said Andy in a hushed voice. "That ought to convince anybody the barn's burning."

They were silent for a moment, listening to the frightening crackle of the flames.

"Jen, when I thought he was going to light the barn on fire," Andy began hesitantly, "all I could think of was wanting to say I was sorry . . . for the way I've been acting."

"It's okay," Jen said into the darkness. "You don't have to apologize."

"I just hate everybody looking at me and talking about me," Andy struggled to explain.

"It's okay," said Jen again. "I know how shy you are. Anyway, my mom says I'm too young for . . . you know . . . that stuff. But we can still be friends." She choked, trying to clear her throat. Her eyes were burning. Smoke was filtering into the barn through its stone walls, and up through the open eaves.

Zeke stamped and whinnied. Caspar shifted nervously and poked his head over the stall door as if to ask, "What's going on?"

"I don't like that smoke," Andy coughed.

"It's not just smoke," Jen gasped. "Andy—look!"

Andy saw something that filled his heart with terror. There was a red glow in the back corner of the roof. The blaze Victor had started outside had reached the new wood rafters under the metal roof. The fire was spreading fast. Soon it would reach the corner posts, then the hay—the whole wood interior of the barn would burst into flames!

Andy twisted his wrists against the bite of the cord that held his hands.

Jen threw him a desperate glance. "Keep trying! We've got to get out of here!" She struggled to reach the knots above her head with her teeth.

Caspar whinnied a warning. Sparks from the roof had ignited the straw beside Zeke's stall. It was only a matter of seconds till it reached the hay where Victor had spilled the gas.

ତ ତ ତ

Meanwhile, Kelsie stood close to Diamond's shoulder aboard the flat barge at the shore. The young mare was tethered to rings along the side of the craft so tightly that she could barely move. Even so, the two smugglers were careful to stay out of her way.

It had taken Kelsie a long time to get Diamond to set foot on the clanging metal deck. Now her eyes were white-rimmed with fear, her ears pinned back, her tail clamped tight to her haunches. She quivered with tension down the whole length of her body.

The smugglers were waiting for Victor to return before heading back to their ship. His kayak and tent were already loaded on the barge.

Kelsie heard hoofbeats in the darkness. A moment later she saw Victor throw himself off Midnight's back and stumble down the rocks to the barge. His face was twisted with emotion.

The bearded man with the British accent man helped him splash aboard. "Did you take care of those kids?" he asked.

"Yes!" Victor exploded. "You tell me to, so I do it!"

"Are you sure?"

"Of course I am sure. I put so much gas on that barn it will soon be a pile of ashes." He pointed to a red glow above the trees to the west. "Look! There is your fire."

"I can smell the smoke from here." The bearded man nodded. "Don't worry. If anyone investigates they'll think some crazy kids fooling around with matches started a fire in an old barn. Accidents happen."

"What will you do with the girl?" Victor jerked his chin toward Kelsie.

"Dump her, once we're in international waters," the man said. "Another accident."

Kelsie sank her head onto the glossy softness of the mare's shoulder. "He set fire to our barn," she whispered to Diamond in horror. "Jen and Andy and the horses are in there. I've got to get off this stupid barge and go help them." But she knew how fast the old barn would burn. Even if she could get away, she would be too late.

"What have I done?" Kelsie murmured. "This is all my fault." By following her wild impulse to meet the woman from the rescue society—by agreeing to take Diamond—she had put herself and her friends in danger. "Aunt Maggie is right," she groaned. "She says I'm reckless and stubborn like my grandmother Elizabeth and I am."

She could hear the shouts of the crew, making last-minute preparations to get underway. They had left Midnight loose on the shore. Kelsie wished she could fly off this barge onto Midnight's back and race away. But it was not going to happen.

◎ ◎ ◎

Back in the blue house on the mainland, Aunt Maggie beamed at Doug and Chrissy. "Seeing you here in the sun porch reminds me of when you were babies. My sister Elizabeth and I used to babysit you, right here in this porch."

"You did?" Doug looked embarrassed. "I don't remember that."

"Of course not." Aunt Maggie sat up straighter and tugged at a pillow. "You were only two years old. One day, I remember, you grabbed Chrissy's little face in both hands and kissed her. Elizabeth and I laughed—it was so dear. We were sure you'd be sweethearts when you grew up, but then my sister drowned, and you went away." Aunt Maggie suddenly sagged back on her pillow and the light went out of her eyes. "I think I'll sleep a little," she said.

Alarmed, Chrissy and Doug watched her slip deep into sleep. Her breathing became ragged.

"Should I call the ambulance?" Doug asked. "Maybe she's having another heart attack."

Chrissy glanced up and nodded. "They can check her out at the hospital, and if she's all right, we'll bring her back home."

Doug hurried to the phone in the kitchen. He was back in a few minutes. "The ambulance is on its way," he told Chrissy. "They said twenty minutes. How is she?"

Chrissy shook her head. "Not any better."

"She seemed so well when we came in," Doug said.

"I'm sure she'll be all right," Chrissy murmured. "But those old memories seem to rock her."

"Some of them rocked me," Doug said. "Imagine us as toddlers in this very room." He reached for Chrissy's hand. "I'm so glad you're here. I would be going crazy alone, with the kids on the island."

"I'm sure they're fine," Chrissy said. "Aunt Maggie's right. Gabriel probably went to check on them."

18

No Way Out

The fire in the barn licked along the edge of the hay bale where the gas had spilled. The fire was gaining force.

"We've got to get out of here!" Andy cried. With the cord cutting into his wrists, he bent as far as he could reach and wiggled at Caspar's stall latch.

"What are you doing?" Jen cried.

"Caspar's the great escape artist, isn't he? If I could get him loose, maybe he could help."

Caspar sensed Andy was trying to free him. He whinnied encouragement, stamping up and down in his eagerness to escape from the stall. A few more wiggles and the bolt slid back. The door swung open. He was free.

"GO, CASPAR!" shouted Andy and Jen together.

At that moment the entire bale of hay burst into flame. It roared like a wildfire, spread to another bale and then another. In a flash, the whole interior of the barn was on fire.

There was no way out through the thick stone walls. The door was the only hope.

Caspar raced toward it. He wheeled and kicked with his powerful hind legs. Smashed against the wood planks. Splintered one board.

"Again!" shouted Andy. "Do it again!"

He and Jen were still tied. Hot, choking smoke filled their lungs and stung their eyes. Even if Caspar kicked down the door and escaped, the two of them were still prisoners. So were the horses, Zeke and Sailor.

But Jen had reached the knots with her teeth—chewed through them. She shook herself free and dashed to undo Andy.

"Get Sailor," she screamed. "I'll get Zeke."

Sailor, sturdy little pony that he was, put his head down and followed Andy out of the stall.

Another splintering crash, and Caspar flattened the door. Air rushed in from outside, fanning the fames. Heat seared his white hide as he dashed out into the night.

Andy turned, looking for Jen and Zeke.

"I can't make Zeke move," he heard Jen shriek. "He's too scared."

"Leave him. You have to come now!" Andy slapped Sailor hard on the butt, heading the pony toward the open door. He turned back. Between him and Jen was a solid wall of flame.

Andy flattened himself to the floor, where the smoke was less intense. He crawled, choking and gasping, to Zeke's stall. He grabbed Jen by the arm and yanked her down beside him. "We have to go," he repeated. "We're going to die."

Just in time, he dragged her away from the stall. With a deafening roar, a section of the roof caved in. The buckled metal and heavy timbers collapsed, burying Zeke's stall under the burning rubble.

"Zeke!" Jen screamed.

"We have to keep going." Andy put his arm around Jen. Keeping low, he kept a firm grip on her and held his breath as he dragged her through the smoke to the open door.

Once through the door, they ran, stumbling and choking, across the pasture, following Caspar and Sailor. All they could think of was getting away from the sights and sounds and smell of the fire. Behind them, burning roof timbers shot sparks high into the air. They were both crying, thinking of Zeke, trapped by the fire.

"He was such a silly, scared horse," sobbed Jen, flinging herself on Caspar's neck. "He couldn't trust me. He never, never trusted anyone, not really."

"Caspar was a hero." Andy stroked his side. "Kelsie would be so proud of him."

"Kelsie!" Jen and Andy both cried at the same time.

"They're going to take her away on the ship—we have to stop them!" Jen scrambled up on Caspar's back. "We'll have to ride to the landing and get your skiff," she panted. "Go to Dark Cove for help."

"It's too late. The smugglers will already be heading out to sea." Andy looked at Jen's smudged, despairing face. "But you're right. We have to try."

He jumped on Sailor's back and got a firm grip on the pony's mane. "Victor says those guys are killers."

☙☙☙

On board the smugglers' small freighter, Kelsie was locked in a box stall built especially for Diamond on the rear deck. She knew at any second Diamond would explode into a frenzy. She would rear and kick and stomp, not caring if she injured herself or anyone else. The trip from shore on the barge had brought the mare to the brink of panic. Hoisting her onto the deck in a sling had sent her over the edge.

Kelsie forced herself to take a deep breath, trying to calm herself. If she was calm, she could regain control of Diamond. Otherwise, she thought, they wouldn't have to worry about how to dispose of her and make it look like an accident. She'd be trampled or kicked to pieces.

She took another deep breath, leaning close to Diamond. Kelsie imagined the mare's foal inside, safe, protected, knowing nothing of what was happening here on the ship. From the men's conversations, Kelsie had learned there were half a dozen crew on board. Most of them didn't speak English. The two men who had come ashore were the leaders, and their usual business was smuggling drugs. They'd brought Victor along because he knew about horses, but none of the other crew members did. They were all afraid of Diamond.

Just then, there was a noise outside the stall. Someone had unlocked the door. It swung open enough to let Victor slip through.

Diamond reared and whinnied, but Victor put a firm hand on her muzzle, settling her. "I came to tell you," he said in a low voice, "your friends are all right."

The light was dim in the stall but Kelsie could see Victor shake his head. "I am not a killer," he said. "I light the fire outside the barn. The horses and your friends will be okay inside."

Kelsie felt her knees sag with relief. Jen and Andy and the horses—alive—and safe! She grabbed Victor's thick, rough hand. "Thank you."

"Do not say anything!" Victor's voice fell lower. "If these men know what I do, they murder me, I am sure. They are very evil. The man who is buying Diamond has connections with people who know these kind of bad people. He hired this ship and this crew. I did not know them before."

"I won't let on," Kelsie whispered her promise. "What I don't understand is how you came to bring Diamond to Saddle Island. How did you know about us—about me?"

"Your friend, Paul Speers talked about you . . ." Victor began.

"He's not my friend!" Kelsie whispered fiercely. Paul Speers had cheated and lied and left Dark Cove with many enemies that summer. But it was true he was part of the thoroughbred racing world. So that's how the meeting had been arranged!

"This man Paul—he is not part of the plan," Victor explained in his harsh whisper. "But he knows the people who own the racing stable where this mare lives. My partner and

I worked in the stable, waiting for her to be bred to the stallion, for the very valuable foal, and we heard him tell about this place, and we think it is perfect." He shuddered. "It is a terrible island. I hope to never see it again!"

"Never mind that," Kelsie said. "What's going to happen to Diamond?"

"We steal her for a man who owes a favor to someone higher up, who owes a favor to someone even higher," Victor explained, with a shrug of his broad shoulders. "At the top there is a rich man who collects the best of everything—the biggest diamond in the world, the best painting by Picasso, the fastest racehorse. That will be Diamond's foal."

"Can you help me get away?" asked Kelsie. "They're going to throw me overboard."

"No." Victor shook his head. "They kill me sure. We are leaving—I must go." He turned and slipped out of the stall.

Somewhere below her, Kelsie heard the deep thump of the ship's engine idling, felt its vibrations in her bones. Ka-thunk, ka-thunk. She had only moments before they powered up and headed out to sea.

Somehow, she had to stop that engine and get off this ship. Kelsie struggled with the stall door. Victor had locked it tight. She looked up. The stall was like a cage, with a strong wire mesh ceiling. The walls were made of plate steel. There was no way out.

19

Go for Help ⊚

Jen slid from Caspar's back at the landing where Andy's skiff bobbed on the rising tide.

"You stay here," Jen told Caspar. She fondled his fuzzy face, leaning her cheek against his. He smelled like smoke. Jen shivered, thinking of their narrow escape. Zeke hadn't been so lucky . . . She felt tears trickle down her cheeks, remembering the beautiful brown horse and her desperate struggle to make him come with her out of that barn.

"No," she said, scrubbing her tears away, "I won't think about Zeke now. There'll be time to be sad later. Now we have to think about Kelsie." She tied Caspar and Sailor to trees near the shore and slipped down the rocks to the skiff.

Andy yanked the starter cord and the motor grumbled into life. He backed the skiff out of the groove in the rock, turned the boat and twisted the throttle to full speed. By now the tide safely covered the old causeway. This was one time he wouldn't have to pick his way among the rocks.

"Jen!" he called to her over the motor's roar, "I don't

think we should head for Dark Cove. It will take too long to explain to our parents what is happening. Dad will never understand. He'll just get mad and yell."

"You're right," Jen called back. "Let's not waste time. Go around the island . . ." She motioned with her arm. "Maybe we can help Kelsie ourselves."

Andy swung the boat around, heading up the channel to the island's north end. As they bumped over the dark swells he shouted, "Did I ever tell you I named this boat the *Jennifer*, after you?"

"No," Jen yelled. "I didn't know she had a name."

"Nobody knows," Andy said.

"I won't tell." Jen patted the side of the boat. After what they had shared tonight, she would never doubt that Andy cared about her. They wouldn't have to talk about it if Andy didn't want to.

After a few minutes at top speed the skiff burst out of the passage between Teapot Island and Saddle Island. Andy slowed the motor. He'd never taken his boat around this end of the island—he knew there were dangerous reefs and a strong current, even when there weren't big swells.

Tough enough in the daylight. Now it was dark. As they headed for the high end of the island, the lights of a boat ahead in the open water confused Andy for a moment.

"Is that the smugglers' ship?" He pointed it out to Jen.

"No, too small, and in the wrong place," she called. "It's a Cape Islander like Gabe's boat, but what would Gabe be doing out here?"

"I don't know, but let's go look. It might be a fishing boat with a radio. They could call for help and we could carry on around the island to look for Kelsie."

Jen nodded her head.

@@@

Steffi LeGrand stood in the living room doorway, looking at the back of her father's bald head. He was stretched out in his reclining chair, watching a hockey game.

"Dad," she said, "I have to tell you something."

"Now?"

"I-I think so. Did you hear that siren a while ago?"

"Yeah." Her dad swiveled his chair around to look at her. "What's the problem?"

"One of my friends says the ambulance went to Maggie Ridout's place."

"Maybe," her father agreed. "I hear she's been sick. What does that have to do with you?"

"Well—nothing," gulped Steffi, "except that Maggie's nephew Doug was looking for Gabriel and I think he wanted Gabe to go out to Saddle Island and get his kids. Doug's, I mean. Maybe it was because Maggie Ridout was, was . . ." Steffi couldn't finish.

Her father popped his chair into an upright position and switched off the TV. "Don't cry!" he said. "I don't understand. Did Gabe go out to look for the kids?"

"No, he couldn't." Steffi drew herself up straight and the words came out in a rush. "Because we, I mean I, played a stupid trick and siphoned the gas out of his boat and he's stuck out there in the cove and I feel awful and I need your help."

Mr. LeGrand's face turned red, then gray. "Stupid doesn't begin . . . how could you? Never mind." He heaved himself out of his chair. "We'd better call Gabe's father."

But there was no answer at the Peters' house. "Come on," Steffi's father said. "Get your coat, girl. We'll have to take our own boat and get some diesel out to that boy."

☙ ☙ ☙

At the same time, on board the smugglers' ship, Kelsie searched Diamond's box stall for a way out. There were flakes of hay and bags of feed piled to one side. That was a bad idea—the smugglers didn't know that a smart horse would soon have a feed bag open and be eating herself sick. Lucky Victor hadn't noticed. She could use that horse feed!

She knew from Andy that the fastest way to wreck an engine and stop a boat was to pollute the fuel. Water would work—or sugar. The crew hadn't left water in the stall. But there was lots of sweet stuff, grain mixed with molasses and pellets of sugar beet fiber.

Kelsie tore open a sack of beet pellets. They looked like broken brown crayons. Kelsie stuffed handfuls of them into her jeans' pockets.

In liquid these pellets would quickly swell, break down into mash. They'd clog up the engine and stop it dead. Kelsie wondered why they'd have high-energy food like beet pulp on board—maybe to make sure Diamond acted like a race-horse when they unloaded her after a long voyage. But it didn't matter why the feed pellets were here. The important thing was to get them into the ship's fuel supply—fast!

First, she had to escape from this stall. Kelsie felt along the walls under the layer of bedding. Steel posts were firmly attached to the deck at the corners, but the wall sections were attached only to those posts. There was a crack at the bottom. At the very back of the stall, where the deck slanted down, where the manure had been piled, Kelsie felt a wider crack.

Could she fit through it? No time to wonder. Kelsie pawed back the wet straw and horse manure, lay down on her back and started to squeeze under the wall. If she got stuck she'd be in a horrible position. Kelsie lay as flat as she could, blew out all her breath and wriggled sideways.

Halfway through, she heard voices.

"Check on the horse, will you?"

Kelsie froze. It was the bearded man with the British accent—the leader. She'd be discovered!

20

Engine Trouble ◉

"Do not disturb that horse. She is quiet now." It was Victor's voice. "She will get agitated again if you go in there."

"All right. But you'd better know what you're doing." Kelsie heard the bearded man stomp away. Victor couldn't know it, but he had saved her from being caught. Her chest was crushed under the stall wall. The bottom of the wall section scraped her face. The smell of horse manure was overpowering.

She had to get out of here! Kelsie gave one last frantic wriggle and burst free on the cold, bare deck. Sucking in an enormous breath, she stood up and tried to brush the worst of the manure and straw off her clothes.

The deck was dimly lit with swinging lightbulbs. In the shadows, Kelsie crept along the side of the hull, searching for the round steel cover of the fuel intake pipe. It should be here—diesel fuel was always pumped in from a hose that went over the side.

The crewmen were forward in the wheelhouse. She could

hear them arguing. They'd be back any minute. Kelsie moved as quickly as she dared and almost tripped over the raised round lid. Unscrewing it, she felt for the pellets in her pockets. She took off the lid and backed away—UGH! The smell of human waste, a hundred times worse than horse manure, rose from the pipe.

Shaking, Kelsie screwed the lid back on. She'd almost wasted her precious pellets on the waste holding tank.

The voices were coming nearer. Kelsie felt frantically for another round cover. She found it, unscrewed it and smelled the sickly sweet odor of diesel fuel. Footsteps were coming closer. Kelsie emptied her pockets into the pipe, stuck the cap back on loosely and pressed herself against the steel hull.

The men went past. Kelsie hid behind a pile of barrels chained to the side of the boat, praying that the beet fiber would clog the engine and shut it down. Soon—before they were far from shore!

@ @ @

The bedside phone's shrill beep woke the old vet, Dr. Bricknell, from his first, deepest sleep. He opened one eye to peer at the clock. Twelve-thirty! Must be some kind of emergency.

But it was just a woman from a racing stable he'd never heard of.

"What are you doing bothering me after midnight?" he thundered into the phone.

"After midnight? Where am I calling?"

"Dark Cove, Nova Scotia," growled the vet.

"Oh! I'm in Kentucky. It's only after ten-thirty here. We must be two hours earlier than you are. I'm so sorry I woke you," the woman apologized.

"Not as sorry as I am. What's this about?"

"Someone called to say you reported finding a thoroughbred mare—possibly pregnant."

"That's right," said Dr. Bricknell.

"Can you describe her?" The woman's voice was eager.

"At this time of night?"

"Sorry. It's important."

Dr. Bricknell sighed. "The mare I examined was about five years old, chestnut, with a white diamond-shaped star on her forehead."

"Interesting. Our five-year-old mare was stolen two weeks ago. She's solid chestnut. No markings." The woman paused. "But markings on a horse can be faked."

"It's been done," agreed the vet. "But do you really think . . ."

The woman interrupted. "The mare's foal will be worth more than half a million dollars. I understand you don't have the number of her tattoo."

"I said I'd check it in the morning." Dr. Bricknell was back to feeling impatient and sleepy. "And I will."

"I'll give you my number," the woman said, and rhymed it off. "Please call back. It's important. There's a sizable reward for information leading to her recovery."

"I'll call you back," Dr. Bricknell promised. "First thing

in the morning. Say eight-thirty. What'll that be? Six-thirty your time?"

"Doesn't matter," the woman told him. "We're always up early to exercise the horses. I'd appreciate it if you'd call. Sorry to have woken you. Goodbye."

Dr. Bricknell hung up. He remembered that it had been hard to read the number on the tattoo. He wondered if someone had tried to tamper with it to make it blurry. It must have been painful for the mare, if they had. He wondered if the diamond on her forehead was more tampering? That could be painful, too. He sighed and rolled over, doubtful it was the same mare. Why would anyone in their right mind steal such a valuable animal and then dump her here in Dark Cove with Kelsie MacKay?

@ @ @

Kelsie huddled against the steel hull, shuddering with cold. Another crew member came aft. She could see him silhouetted against the light. He rattled the door of Diamond's stall. "You still alive in there, kid?"

Kelsie thought her heart would stop.

At that moment the engine below thudded into vigorous life. They were heading out to sea. Ka-thump, ka-thump, ka-thump. The ship began to move, the propeller churning through the water. Kelsie thought of the fuel pouring into the engine, burning. When would the beet pellets work? When would the engine choke?

The crewman was opening the stall door. Diamond let out

a whinny of defiance and fear. Her hooves thudded against the stall wall.

"Hey!" the man called. "The kid's not here!" He slammed the door shut again.

More footsteps came running.

Kelsie cowered against the hull. Light shone in her eyes. "There she is!"

Rough hands reached out to grab her. "How did you get out?" the crew member demanded, dragging her over to Diamond's stall. "The stall was locked tight."

As if in answer, Diamond's hooves crashed against the metal door, making the crewman jump back in alarm.

Kelsie said nothing.

"Devil horse," the man muttered. "And now a female on board. Bad luck. Cursed ship."

He bellowed at Kelsie above the thudding of the engine and the crash of Diamond's kicking. "Get moving! I'm taking you to the boss." Poking and prodding her from behind, he forced her forward.

At that instant, the engine fell still. There was a moment of total silence on the ship, as if everyone was waiting for it to burst back into life. When it didn't, footsteps pounded down the deck. Orders were barked out.

"Get that engine compartment open!"

"Get that engine started!"

In the confusion, Kelsie was temporarily forgotten. She watched while crewmen ran back and forth with lights and tools. The smugglers were not patient. They shouted threats at the engine mechanic, yelling at him to hurry up.

No one but Kelsie noticed that the ship was drifting fast toward the northeast.

She suddenly realized they were in danger from more than a disabled engine. Out there, just off Saddle Island, was the reef of jagged rocks called the Five Sisters. Kelsie remembered it clearly from the map of the island in her room. Dozens of shipwrecks were marked on the Five Sisters. One of them had been her grandparents' fishing boat.

She glanced at the dark sea. Big swells from yesterday's wind were sweeping the freighter closer and closer to the reef.

Kelsie opened her mouth to shout a warning, then snapped it shut. Sinking the ship might give her and Diamond one last chance. She moved as quietly as she could toward the stall. If she could just get the door unlatched she'd be able to let Diamond out when the moment came.

She reached for the latch but a strong hand gripped her shoulder. She whipped around and saw the bearded smuggler, the man who had ordered Victor to get rid of Jen and Andy. Rage welled up inside her. "Let go of me!"

"What do you think you're doing now?" he snarled.

"I want to check on Diamond." Kelsie held her ground.

"How did you get out here?" The man's eyes were cold and hard.

"I squeezed under the wall."

"Impossible."

"Possible. I'm here. Someone left Diamond's food in

the stall. She could eat it all, swell up and die. Is that what you want?"

The man swore. Holding Kelsie by the collar of her jacket, he banged open the latch on the stall door with his other hand. "Go on—get the feed," he ordered.

21

The Five Sisters ⊚

As soon as the stall latch was open, Diamond lunged out the door. Expecting this, Kelsie twisted out of her way. The bearded smuggler wasn't so lucky. Diamond's fleeing body knocked him to the deck and one of her flying feet caught him a glancing blow in the ribs. He doubled over, howling with pain.

Kelsie raced after Diamond. This was their chance!

But Victor dashed toward the mare, grasping at the side of the ship to keep his balance. He grabbed Diamond by the halter and wrestled with the frantic horse, trying to control her.

"You!" he shouted at the bearded man, his fear of the smuggler forgotten in his anger. "Why you open the stall?"

"The kid." The smuggler gripped his side. "She said we should get the mare's feed away from her, or she'd get sick."

"The girl played a trick on you!" Victor cried.

"Where is she?" the bearded man howled. "Find her!"

Kelsie dodged behind the barrels where she had hidden before. It was only a matter of seconds before Victor would slam Diamond back in her stall and they'd find her. She felt for the chain that fastened the barrels. Fumbling, struggling with the heavy steel links that hooked it to the hull, she slid it loose. Held it tight. Waited.

"There she is!" Another crewman had spotted her.

"Get her!" the bearded man howled.

Half a dozen men converged on the back deck, reaching for Kelsie over the barrels.

She let go of the chain.

The heavy barrels, released, sprang into motion with the roll of the ship. As the men charged at Kelsie, the barrels struck them at their knees, knocking them down like bowling pins.

Kelsie knew she had only delayed her capture. She glanced over the side of the ship at the dark swirling water, which foamed and curled around sharp, pointed rocks. They had drifted onto the Five Sisters.

As the men kicked the barrels aside and grabbed for her, the ship struck the rocks with a sickening crunch. The deck tipped violently sideways. Kelsie fell against the hull with a thud. Victor and the other crew members were totally unprepared. They stumbled on the slanting deck, shouting.

"What has happened?" Victor's voice rose above the cries of the other men.

"You've run aground!" Kelsie screamed back. "You're on a reef!"

She saw the fair-haired smuggler working his way toward them down the deck. His face was a mask of rage and fear.

"The engine is clogged with some kind of sludge," he cried. "When I find the person who did this . . . !"

Too late. The ship gave a violent heave and slid backward. "We're sinking," shouted the bearded man. "Abandon ship!"

The crew members scrambled for the emergency supplies at the front of the ship. By now, the bow was high in the air. Water slopped over the stern.

"What about the horse?" Victor was still holding Diamond's rope. The deck was on a steep slant and they were sliding backward.

"Shoot it! And the kid." The fair-haired man pulled a gun out of his waistband and pointed it at Diamond's head. "No witnesses!"

"Not the horse!" Victor leaped forward and knocked the gun out of the man's hand. The gun spun into the air and splashed into the sea.

"You . . . !" The fair-haired man lunged at Victor and grabbed him but was stopped in his tracks by a shout from the boss.

"Let him go. And let the wretched beast and the girl go down with the ship." He clutched his ribs where Diamond had kicked him. "I can't walk. Help me get to the bow. We have to save our own skins."

For a second, the fair-haired man looked confused. Then he let go of Victor and reached down for the injured man, who was still hunched over on the deck. They struggled toward the ship's bow.

Kelsie grabbed Diamond's rope. "Thank you, Victor," she said. "You saved Diamond."

"It is no use." Victor shook his head. "The horse will never reach the shore—she is too tired to swim." He clung to the ship's side, which was now as steeply angled as a flight of stairs. "I must try to get in lifeboat, if they take me." He turned his back on Kelsie and Diamond and pulled himself up the deck toward the bow, where the inflatable life rafts were being launched.

At that moment the stern of the ship was smothered by a huge swell. Kelsie and Diamond were swept off the deck and into the ocean. The water closed over Kelsie's head.

☙ ☙ ☙

Steffi LeGrand and her father had sped across the swells rolling into Dark Cove in their powerboat, heading for the *Suzanne*'s running lights, far out in the cove. But when they'd reached the boat there was no answer to their shouts, no Gabe running on deck to catch their rope.

"He's gone!" Steffi said after they searched the wheelhouse and the dark space below decks. "What's happened to him?"

Her father's face was creased with worry. "We'll have to take the *Suzanne* back to the cove ourselves. Start a search for the boy." He swung into the wheelhouse. "I don't know what you were thinking of—sending Gabriel out here with an empty fuel tank! You'd just better hope, young lady, that he is not in serious trouble."

"I can't die," Kelsie's brain shrieked as she struggled in the dark water. "Not here on the Five Sisters where my grand-parents drowned. Aunt Maggie would never for—GULP—give me!"

She coughed out the mouthful of seawater she'd swallowed. Where was Diamond? Had she already gone under? No, there was her head, above water, not far . . . A few strokes brought her to the mare's side. Diamond wasn't struggling. She wasn't swimming. She was just standing there calmly with the waves washing over her back.

"STANDING!" Kelsie's brain screamed again. "She's standing up." Diamond must be on a rock. Kelsie held her breath and went under. Her feet touched bottom almost instantly. The water was over her head, but not over Diamond's. She went under again and felt ahead. Swam a few strokes and felt again.

They seemed to be on a granite ledge, sloping upward, toward the shore. The same rock formations as on the land.

"Diamond," Kelsie gasped, swimming back to her. "I think you can walk. Come on, girl, there's the shore—nice solid rock. Just walk, come on, you can do this."

◙ ◙ ◙

Gabe shone his powerful flashlight on the water ahead and to the left. "I can't see anything!" he called back to Andy and Jen.

Gabe had radioed the coast guard from the *Suzanne* and

jumped into the skiff as soon as he heard what had happened. As they came around the end of the island they had watched the smugglers' ship strike the rocks, seen her lights tip, then fade out. For almost half an hour they'd searched the dark ocean, afraid they were too late.

"I don't understand how the smugglers ran aground on the rocks," Gabe shouted over the motor's roar. "They must know the Five Sisters if they've been here before."

"I'll bet Kelsie had something to do with it," said Andy, slowing the engine as they approached the reef of rocks. "My crazy big sister wouldn't just stand by and let them take her and Diamond away without a fight."

"You're right," Jen agreed. She huddled on the middle seat, paralyzed with fear for Kelsie.

Gabe continued to search the water with his light. "I'd like to get my hands on the guys who kidnapped her." He shook his head. "If only Steffi and her friends hadn't siphoned my fuel, I would have been on the island—I could have done something."

"I hope . . ." Andy began, "I hope she's all right. If anything happens to my sister—"

"Don't worry," Gabe shouted. "The coast guard will be on its way by now."

But Jen heard the doubt in Gabe's voice. She knew the coast guard station was far down the shore. The smugglers' ship had sunk ages ago. What if they came too late?

A few hopeless minutes later, Andy twisted the throttle, suddenly cutting the engine dead.

"What are you doing?" Jen asked.

"Can't hear anything with this outboard," he muttered. "Want to listen."

All they could hear was the faraway boom of the waves hitting the shore of Saddle Island, a higher hiss and the crash of swells striking the rocks of the Five Sisters. Andy cupped his hands around his mouth and bellowed, "Kelsie! Are you out there?"

A distant cry came over the water. "Did you hear that?" He stared through the darkness. Gabe said, "N-no."

Jen shook her head. "There's nothing, Andy."

"Listen," Andy insisted. "I thought I heard something. KEL-SIE!" he hollered again.

This time they all heard it, a weak cry for help.

Andy yanked the engine cord so hard he almost tore his arm out of its socket. The engine coughed into life and then roared as Andy pulled the control to the right and headed into shore.

A few minutes later they caught sight of Kelsie and the horse in Gabe's flashlight beam. Diamond had come ashore on a piece of coastline where the rocks slanted steeply into the water. The area was sheltered from the worst of the pounding surf, but there was no way a tired horse could climb those slippery rocks to safety. Each wave washed her cruelly close, then sucked her out again before she could get any footing.

"Help us!" Kelsie cried frantically.

Gabe turned to Andy. "Pull up the skiff. Then come give us a hand." He jumped over the side as the skiff landed and then plunged through the water to Kelsie's side. Her wet hair hung in her face, and her voice was hoarse from screaming at Diamond. She threw one arm around his neck. "Oh, Gabe," she cried. "I'm so glad you're here. Poor Diamond! I can't get her up these rocks." She looked past his shoulder. "Where's the *Suzanne*?"

"Don't ask," Gabe said. "Just get ready to push on this horse when the next wave comes."

Andy and Jen had dragged the skiff above the reach of the waves and now came scrambling over the rocks and splashing through the shallows between them to help.

"All together, when I say," yelled Gabe. "NOW!"

The wave swept in. Shoving and pulling and shouting encouragement, the four of them heaved Diamond up onto the rocks. Kelsie, shaking with cold and relief, hugged the mare's slender neck as they led her to more level ground. Her elegant head drooped. "It's all over," Kelsie promised. "No more water. You're safe now."

Diamond didn't lift her head.

"Come on," Kelsie urged the mare. "Let's go and find Midnight. She's somewhere on this shore."

22

Last Night on Saddle Island ◉

The coast guard vessel tossed on the high tide. Its powerful searchlight swept the rocks along the shore.

"Identify yourselves," a voice boomed from the boat. "We can see your lights."

"It's Gabriel Peters," Gabe shouted back.

"Glad you're all right, Gabe! We've been looking for you—your boat turned up in Dark Cove."

"I've got Kelsie and Andy MacKay and Jennifer Morrisey with me. Can you let their folks know they're okay?"

"Will do, but we can't pick you up this time," the voice boomed again. "We've got a full load of thugs from a couple of lifeboats. Have to turn them over to the authorities. We'll come back for you."

"That's okay," Gabe hollered. "We've got a skiff."

"I hear you." The rumble of the boat's engines turned into a roar as it sped out to sea.

Gabe wrapped his jacket around Kelsie's shoulders. "Come on. Let's get in Andy's skiff and go home. I want to find out how the *Suzanne* got to Dark Cove—make sure she's all right."

Kelsie stared up at him. "W-what about the h-horses?" she asked, trying to keep her teeth from chattering.

"They'll be all right here for one night!"

"No, they won't," Kelsie insisted stubbornly. "Diamond has been through so much, I'm worried she might lose her f-foal. And we can't leave Midnight and Caspar and Sailor and Zeke roaming around the island."

"You kids and your . . . horses!" Gabe exploded.

"They're our r-responsibility," Kelsie stammered.

"But you're soaking wet and freezing."

"We've got dry clothes and camping gear over at the landing," said Jen.

"We'll warm up, walking across the island," Andy added.

Gabe sighed, and gave in. They pulled Andy's skiff far above the high tide mark and secured her to a boulder. She'd be safe there until morning.

Kelsie stared out at the dark open ocean. "I hope Victor made it into one of the lifeboats," she said to Andy. "He told me how he saved you guys by faking the barn fire, and then he stopped the smugglers from shooting at me and Diamond."

Andy swallowed hard. Kelsie thought everything was all right now. How were they ever going to tell her the barn was destroyed, and Zeke with it?

They headed down the shore, searching for Midnight.

@@@

Midnight had stayed close to Victor's campsite. "What a good horse you are," Kelsie murmured, stroking her neck. "You waited here and trusted we'd come for you."

Nothing was left of the campsite but scattered stones and a black stain on the rock where Victor's fire had burned. "You'd never know he was here," said Kelsie. "It's as if the whole thing never happened."

"That's how the smugglers work," muttered Gabe. "They come and go without leaving any trace behind."

They set out along the old road that ringed the island. Keeping up with Gabe's long stride warmed Kelsie and suited Diamond. As they left the boom of the waves behind, the mare's head came up and her body settled into an easy rhythm.

"Isn't she a wonderful horse?" Kelsie sighed. "She's sensitive and intelligent, but brave, too." She described Diamond bursting out of her stall on the ship, knocking the smuggler aside. "She really saved herself," she said proudly.

"How did the smugglers get wrecked on the Five Sisters?" Andy asked. "Weren't they headed out to sea?"

"Well, I knew I had to stop the ship and get off," Kelsie explained. "I remembered what you said about never letting anything get in the gas tank or the engine would seize up, so I found something that would do it."

Gabe laughed when she described dumping beet pellets

into the fuel tank. "You weren't the only one in the business of stopping ships tonight," he said. He told her about running out of fuel and his suspicions that Steffi was guilty of siphoning his diesel.

"What a crazy coincidence." Kelsie shrugged deeper into Gabe's jacket. "But why would Steffi want to stop the *Suzannne*?"

Gabe hesitated. "Who knows? She was mad because I wouldn't go to the Clam Shack with her and her friends." He paused again. "I was worried about you kids out on the island at night—I'd seen the smugglers' light and I wanted to make sure you were all right. But Steffi has this crazy idea that I like you . . . as more than a friend. As if! You're only a kid."

Kelsie could hear the exasperation in Gabe's voice. He didn't know how much he was hurting her feelings. Thirteen for now, she thought. You just wait, Gabriel Peters.

Jen said, "So I guess Steffi won't be too pleased when she finds out you're spending the night with us on the island."

"Maybe not." Gabe sounded embarrassed. "Her trick sort of backfired, didn't it?"

The trek across the island seemed to take forever. When they reached the cutoff trail to the old farm, Kelsie smelled smoke. "That must have been a huge fire Victor made," she said. "It's lucky he didn't burn down the whole barn!"

Midnight snorted in alarm and Diamond whinnied as if she agreed. Andy reached for Jen's hand. They had to tell Kelsie the truth!

@ @ @

By the time they reached the other side of the island Kelsie was staggering with exhaustion. But Diamond looked like a young horse again. Her head flew up and her ears pricked forward when she heard Caspar's welcoming whinny. She pulled on her rope, trying to reach the spot where he and Sailor were tied to the trees.

"Where's Zeke?" Kelsie asked.

Andy gulped. "Zeke didn't make it—"

"What do you mean?" Alarm swept through Kelsie. She gripped Diamond's rope as if her life depended on it.

"The whole barn caught on fire after Victor set the fire outside." Andy forced the words out. "We . . . Jen . . . tried."

"If it hadn't been for Caspar, none of us would have got out," Jen said in a low voice. "He kicked down the door. But Zeke—wouldn't come."

Kelsie stumbled over to Caspar, tears blinding her. She stroked his rough cheek. "Thank you," she murmured. "Oh! Poor Zeke." Her stomach churned. "That's why we could still smell smoke when we came past the cutoff to the farm."

"The barn is gone, Kel," Jen said. She came and put her arm around Kelsie's shaking shoulders.

Kelsie shook her head, unable to speak. All she could think of was handsome, skittery Zeke, how hard he tried to do things right, even though he was anxious and worried all the time—how beautiful he looked trotting across the pasture. "It's all ruined," she sobbed. "The barn and the spring and the old farm—our dream, our horse refuge, everything we've worked for this summer."

"I'm sorry, kids," Gabe said. "But we could rebuild the barn."

There was a long silence.

"I'm not sure keeping horses on Saddle Island is a good idea," Kelsie finally said. "Diamond needs a vet, and we won't be able to get her to the mainland until you get fuel for the *Suzanne*, and the tide's high enough to bring her into the landing, and . . ."

"Time to think about all that later," Gabe interrupted. "Right now, we could all use some food, and maybe a couple of hours' sleep. It's already four in the morning."

They built an enormous fire, ate sandwiches, drank hot chocolate and set up the tent with the door facing the warm blaze. Kelsie, Andy and Jen squeezed inside. Gabe rolled up in blankets near the fire.

But Kelsie couldn't sleep. When the rest of them were deep asleep, she slipped out of the tent and went to check on Diamond. "How are you doing, girl," she whispered. "It'll soon be light."

Diamond neighed softly. She had stopped shivering and seemed to be resting with Caspar nearby. He's like Gabe, Kelsie thought. Like a big brother to Diamond.

She walked down to the edge of the water and looked up. The sky had cleared and millions of stars glittered over the cove. As if the ocean were a mirror, sparkles of biolumines-cent plankton lit the water. It was so beautiful that Kelsie held her breath. She sat down on the rocks to watch.

Weariness swept over her like one of the waves that rose and fell on the shore. She was falling asleep with her eyes open. She thought she dreamed she heard a sound behind her, turned and saw a shape walk out of the blackberry bushes that arched over the trail to the old farm.

From where she sat it looked like the ghost of a horse, walking slowly, head down, toward her.

"Zeke?" Kelsie called sleepily.

The apparition lifted its head. It came forward, limping, into the clearing. The firelight's glow showed a glimpse of dark brown.

Kelsie came fully awake with a jolt. "Zeke!" she screamed.

Gabe shot up from his blanket. The door to the tent burst open and Jen and Andy scrambled out.

The horse limped over to the other horses and they greeted him with low whickers.

"Zeke!" Jen ran to him in her bare feet. He lowered his head, poking in her pocket for a carrot. "You're all right— oh, poor boy, you're hurt. Your leg!" She was sobbing and laughing at the same time. "He's going to be okay."

The rest of them surrounded her and Zeke.

"He's alive." Andy shook his head. "He must have raced after us and gone the other way in the woods. But he remembered the landing and came back here—"

"This calls for a celebration!" Gabe said. "I'm going to build up the fire."

Kelsie stood back, watching. The stars and the fire and her friends and the horses held her in a moment of joy so fierce she knew she would always remember it.

23

Dr. Bricknell's News @

Five and a half hours later they were awakened by the scrape of a boat's keel on the sand.

Gabe untangled himself from his blanket outside the tent. It was the *Suzanne*!

He expected to see his father's angry face on board. Instead, it was Steffi's dad who peered at him from the deck. Steffi jumped ashore with the *Suzanne*'s rope in her hand and a sheepish look on her face. Her hair was limp and straggly, her makeup streaked and she clearly hadn't slept all night.

"Steffi!" Gabe said.

Kelsie burst out of the tent behind him. "And Dr. Bricknell!" she shouted, blinking in astonishment as the vet climbed awkwardly ashore. "How did you know we needed you?"

"Had my own reasons for coming—need to take a look at that thoroughbred mare you've got," he hollered back.

"Couldn't get here any sooner," Mr. LeGrand called. "Not enough water between these islands at low tide."

Kelsie glanced at her watch. If it wasn't low tide, what

time was it? Ten-thirty! They'd slept in.

Steffi was walking toward them. She stared at Kelsie, and then at the rumpled blanket where Gabe had slept. "I'm— I'm sorry, Gabriel." She stumbled over her words. "I'm so glad you're all right. Last night, when we couldn't find you on the *Suzanne*, I was afraid . . ."

Gabe hardly looked at her. He was already striding down to his boat to check her over.

Jen and Andy emerged from the tent as the vet reached their campsite.

"I promised a woman I'd have a look at that mare's tattoo," Dr. Bricknell explained to Kelsie. "I went by your place but your dad said the mare was out here, so I hitched a ride on the *Suzanne*." He looked from Kelsie to Andy. "He also told me your Aunt Maggie had to go to the hospital last night. She's okay, they brought her back, but he'd like you both home as soon as you can make it."

Andy scrubbed at his spiky blond hair. "Poor Aunt Maggie."

Kelsie said, "We'll come right away, but first can you take a look at Zeke and Diamond? They both had a hard night."

"That's what I'm here for." The vet climbed up the landing rocks to the horses grazing near the trees.

Kelsie and Jen went with him, telling him about some of the horses' adventures the night before.

First he checked Zeke. "Minor burns, except for that left foreleg," he said. "That'll want some watching. Must have been quite a fire." He gave Kelsie and Jen a questioning look.

"The barn—" Jen began, but Dr. Bricknell had already turned his attention to Diamond.

He walked all around the mare, looking at her from every angle. Then he stepped up close to her head, rubbed his fingers across the diamond on her forehead and said, "Hmm."

What did that mean, Kelsie wondered. She watched anxiously as he listened to Diamond's heart and belly, felt her gums, pinched a fold of skin on her shoulder, felt carefully up and down each leg and along her back.

"Seems sound," he announced. "A little stiffness in her back, but nothing rest won't cure. What have you children been up to?"

Kelsie was so filled with relief she couldn't answer. "Are you sure her foal's okay, too?" she asked instead.

"Don't see why there should be a problem," the vet said kindly. "This foal's not going to be born till spring next year, you know. It's not like it's coming tomorrow."

"That's good." Kelsie sank down on the mossy ground. "I hope I can keep her and her baby."

The vet pulled a notepad and pen out of his shirt pocket. "I wouldn't count on that. This lady that phoned from Kentucky thinks you might have a mare that was stolen from her. I've got to write down the number of her tattoo and call her back."

"Kentucky!" Kelsie jumped to her feet in surprise.

"That's right. And if it is her mare, she's carrying a foal worth a lot of money. She was bred to Peregrine, the Triple Crown winner."

"But what makes her think—?" Kelsie went to stand beside Diamond as Dr. Bricknell peered at the tattoo inside her lip.

The vet wrote down the number of the tattoo. "This mare matches the description the woman gave me, except that her horse doesn't have a white diamond-shaped star," he muttered. He rubbed Diamond's forehead again. The mare snorted and backed up. "The skin is a bit tender," he said, "and some of the hair seems to be falling out. Could be bleached, or a dye."

"You mean Diamond doesn't have a diamond?" Kelsie stroked her glossy shoulder.

"Maybe not." Dr. Bricknell closed his notebook. "The tattoo will tell us. I'd better hurry and make that call. Are you coming back to town on Gabriel's boat?"

"Uh—I guess so," Kelsie managed to stammer. Dr. Bricknell's news fit with what the smugglers had said. Of course she wouldn't be able to keep Diamond if she belonged to somebody, if she and her foal were so valuable.

She glanced at Jen, who was gently patting Zeke's long nose. "The horses will be okay here, for a while," Kelsie said. "We don't want to take them back to the pasture, do we, Jen?"

"No," said Jen. "I'm sure this guy won't want to go near the farm for a long time."

"Let's get going," Gabe called from his boat. "We can come back for Andy's skiff and the rest of this stuff later."

Kelsie and Jen tethered Diamond and Zeke with the other

horses. There was lots of grass to eat and all kinds of bushes to nibble on. Kelsie leaned her head on Caspar's cheek. "You look after everything, big guy. I'm leaving you in charge, as usual. And please don't get any ideas about getting loose and swimming after us. We need you to take care of Diamond and Sailor and Midnight—and Zeke!"

@ @ @

While they waited for the news about Diamond, they had breakfast at the blue house. Jen's mom, Chrissy, flipped pancakes, while Doug poured juice for everybody.

"They've adjusted Aunt Maggie's medication and I was able to bring her home last night," Doug explained. "I'm sure she'd like to see you, Kelsie and Andy, but one at a time."

Kelsie went first. The sun was streaming through the sun porch windows, shining on Aunt Maggie's bed. She sat straight up, her pillows neat, her gray hair pulled back in two silver clips. Some of the pink was back in her cheeks and a tangle of bright wool was spread across her lap.

"Hi," Kelsie said. "How are you feeling?"

"Much better. It turns out they were giving me too much of something and not enough of something else. Crazy Dr.s!"

"Can I help untangle your wool?" Kelsie asked.

"No, it's a one-person job." Aunt Maggie shook her head. "You can't get impatient and pull the wool or it gets worse." Her long, strong fingers gently separated the strands of green and purple and blue. "When I'm feeling stronger I'd like to start hooking a new rug. Maybe with a picture of Saddle Island on it."

There was a pause. Then Kelsie said, "Aunt Maggie, we had a fire last night. The barn burned and one of the horses almost died."

"Is the barn . . . did it burn down?" asked her aunt.

"Yes. I didn't see it, but Jen said . . ." Kelsie put her head down on her aunt's patchwork quilt. "I don't think I ever want to keep horses on the island again."

Aunt Maggie reached out and stroked Kelsie's tangled curls. "It's a strange thing about islands," she said. "There are hundreds of them along this Eastern Shore—maybe thousands, if you count the small ledges. The Indians used them for fishing and clamming. Once we found a place where an old tree had fallen over and in its roots were layers and layers of shells from Indian camps long ago. Then the fishermen tried to claim them, and farmers like your great-great-grandfather Ridout settled on them. Almost every island has stone foundations and root cellars. Some have roses and springs like Saddle Island, and graveyards, too."

Kelsie sat up. Her aunt's eyes had a faraway look. "I don't think the islands ever belong to us," she said. "They belong to themselves. They're wonderful places to visit and spend some time, but they tend to break your heart if you claim them for your own. And they hold their secrets close."

Kelsie nodded. Aunt Maggie was right. She'd almost drowned off the island, but she'd never tell her aunt that.

Her aunt returned to the task of untangling her wool. "Just

because you give up the island doesn't mean you have to give up your dream of a horse refuge," she said. "There's plenty of room right here on the mainland. You can bring Caspar, and that pony, and the Canadian mare, and the racehorse too, if you like."

Kelsie wanted to hug Aunt Maggie, but she was afraid of crushing her. "Thanks, Aunt Maggie," she said. "I'll go tell Andy he can come and see you."

Her aunt lifted her eyes from her work as Kelsie stood up. She said, "You know, you look like my sister Elizabeth, but really you're not so much like her."

Kelsie stood frozen to the spot. "I'm . . . not?" she managed to ask.

"No," Aunt Maggie went on, "you're much more independent, more grown-up than Elizabeth was at your age. You've had to be, moving around the country, taking care of Andy and your father after your mother died. Of course, you love horses just like she did, but you're very much your own person."

Kelsie smiled at her aunt. "I'm glad you told me that," she said. "I'll go get Andy."

24

Kelsie's Reward ☙

Dr. Bricknell brought the news an hour later. He screeched to a stop outside the blue house and burst into the kitchen.

"The mare's real name is Bye Bye Blues," he announced. "Stable name, Bizzy."

Kelsie sighed. "Bizzy. That suits her better than Diamond. Are you sure?"

"Very sure," said the vet. "Her owners are arranging horse transport for her, and one of them, Julie Petruzzi, is flying up from Kentucky to check her out personally."

"I hate to let Diamond—I mean, Bizzy—go," Kelsie said. "We'll never get to see her baby."

"What do you think the horse smugglers were going to do with the foal?" asked Jen. All four of them were sitting around Aunt Maggie's kitchen table. "It would never be able to race without registration papers and a tattoo of his own."

"That's right." Dr. Bricknell shrugged. "Perhaps they were going to fake those, too. Or perhaps the man who wanted him arranges private races with other horse owners. Or maybe he just likes to collect the finest things in the world."

"Horses aren't things," muttered Kelsie.

"They certainly are not." The vet pushed back his chair and stood up. "So it's good you rescued his mother. Gabriel told me some of what happened last night on the ship."

"Shh!" Kelsie put her finger to her lips. "My dad doesn't know."

The Dr. smiled, then spoke in a whisper. "Apparently, the coast guard saved the miserable hides of the ship's crew and the horse thief. Gabriel got a message and thought you'd like to know—the authorities have been trying to catch the smugglers for a while. There are going to be some serious consequences for those fellows . . ."

"We'll have to put in a good word for Victor," said Kelsie. "He did try to help."

Dr. Bricknell leaned forward to whisper another message. "Did I tell you the owner mentioned quite a large reward for Bizzy's safe return?"

"A reward?" Kelsie and Jen jumped to their feet.

"How much?" asked Andy.

"They mentioned a figure in the high five figures—for her safe return." Dr. Bricknell's lined face broke into a rare smile.

"Then we'd better find Gabe and see if he can bring Bizzy over while the tide's high." Kelsie grabbed her jacket from the back of the chair. "Thanks, Dr. Bricknell. Come on, you two."

That evening, as the sun went down behind Dark Cove, a beautiful silver horse van, pulled by a large pickup, rolled down Aunt Maggie's driveway. It was fitted out for a queen, with a slanted stall, padded floor and large windows.

Bizzy would only ride in it as far as the Halifax airport, where a private jet was waiting to fly her back to Kentucky.

Julie Petruzzi, Bizzy's owner, led her out of Aunt Maggie's barn. She was draped in an expensive purple horse blanket. Her expression was calm and alert, every flick of her ears aristocratic.

Kelsie and Jen stood, speechless. Was this the tough little mare that they'd ridden through dark brush, swum in rough water?

"I have to thank you so much for taking care of Bizzy," Julie said.

"How did she get stolen?" Kelsie asked.

"It was well planned. Shortly after we were certain Bizzy was expecting Peregrine's foal, we hired two new stable hands. They had excellent references." She paused and shook her head. "One of them was Victor, the man you met. The other, Sandy, disappeared the day Bizzy disappeared from the brood mare barn. They haven't found him yet."

Julie stopped on Aunt Maggie's lawn to admire the view. "What a beautiful spot," she sighed. "It's so peaceful. It looks like nothing bad could ever happen here."

Kelsie and Jen shared a glance. Julie wouldn't think Dark

Cove was so peaceful if she'd been around last night, they were thinking. Smugglers, and fires, and shipwrecks. They'd told Julie as little as possible about her mare's terrible experience. The police would fill her in with the details later.

In the meantime, Bizzy looked like a horse who didn't have a care in the world. Jen and Kelsie had brushed and groomed her till she shone after her voyage in Gabe's boat.

"Well," Julie said. "I hate to go, but we have a plane to catch." She handed Kelsie an envelope. "This doesn't even begin to express my gratitude, but I hope it comes in handy."

Just then there was a loud whinny from the barn. They all looked up.

"That's Caspar," said Kelsie. "He wants to say goodbye." She sprinted back to the barn and led Caspar out of his stall and across the lawn to touch noses with Bizzy.

"He doesn't know anything about her having a different name and going on a plane," Jen murmured. "But he knows about trailers and he knows he's going to lose a friend."

"Goodbye, Bizzy," Kelsie whispered, stroking the mare's smooth cheek. "We'll miss you."

Back in the kitchen they all sat staring at the check in the middle of the table. "So much money," Kelsie said. "Sixty-five thousand. Do you think it's real?"

"It's real, all right," her dad said, "and it's yours. Put it in the bank for your education."

"I don't know," Kelsie said. "It wasn't just me who saved Diamond, I mean Bizzy. We all helped. Anyway, college is a long way away."

She looked around at them. "I've been thinking. We need to stick around and look after Aunt Maggie until she's completely better. You need a job, Dad, and so does Jen's mom. Plus, Andy and I want to stay in Dark Cove. We don't want to move. So here's my idea. Listen . . ."

๑ ๑ ๑

On the kind of beautiful warm morning that sometimes comes to Nova Scotia in early April, Kelsie came rushing into the Clam Shack waving a large envelope. "It's from Julie!" she squealed. "Sent by special courier. Must be a picture of Bizzy's foal!"

She brushed right past Steffi, who was sitting two stools down from Gabe, throwing him longing glances, but not daring to start up a conversation. He hadn't forgotten the trick she'd played on his boat.

Jen wiped her hands on her apron and reached across the counter for Kelsie's envelope. "Andy, Mom, come and look!" she called through the kitchen door.

There had been some changes to the Clam Shack since September. With some of Kelsie's reward money, her dad had made a down payment on the restaurant and hired Chrissy as head cook. Kelsie, Jen and Andy all worked there after school and on weekends.

On this Saturday morning, the restaurant was busy, as usual. There were plans to expand the Clam Shack—make space to sell local crafts like Aunt Maggie's rugs. On top of that, Doug MacKay was buying a Cape Islander to take tourists out to watch whales and birds and seals. Andy was so excited about the new boat he could hardly wait for summer to start.

Kelsie, Andy and her mom crowded around Jen as she pulled a large color photograph from the envelope. "Look! Isn't he gorgeous?" They'd had a call from Julie a week before saying the foal had been born and it was a colt.

Gabe slid off his stool and peered over Kelsie's shoulder.

"He's going to be a great racehorse," sighed Kelsie. "He looks just like his mother, chestnut all over."

Jen turned the photo over and read: "Here's the first picture of Bizzy's foal, taken a few hours after his birth. Already looks like a winner."

"What's his name?" Andy asked.

"It says here his name is Seabird," Jen read. "Julie says she wanted 'bird' in the name for his father and 'sea' because of his mother's adventure before he was even born. She says it will bring him luck."

"Seabird won't need luck," Kelsie sighed. "Not with a mother like Diamond, I mean Bizzy. That mare has so much heart . . ." She shut her eyes, remembering.

"What's all the excitement?" Steffi came to look at the photo. "Cute," she said. She glanced up at Gabe. "Any chance you're coming to the school dance next week?"

"Not sure." Gabe gave her a cold stare. "Maybe."

Steffi turned and walked away.

"Come on." Jen nudged Gabe's arm. "You have to forgive her some time. At least she's stopped acting like you're her private property."

Gabe shrugged and reached for the foal's picture. "I'll think about it in a few years, about the time this colt wins the Kentucky Derby." He grinned and changed the subject. "How's the addition to the barn at the blue house coming along?" he asked Kelsie.

"Almost done," Kelsie sighed happily. "There's room for Caspar, Zeke, Midnight, Sailor and even a couple of other horses." She glanced out the window. "Speaking of the horses, I'd like to go for a ride on the beach—it's such a nice day. Want to come, Jen?"

"Sure!" Jen whipped off her apron. "Can you spare us for a couple of hours, Mom?"

"Of course," her mother said. "It's Saturday, and you shouldn't waste this weather."

A few minutes later they were racing down the white sand beach, Kelsie on Caspar, and Jen on Zeke. His burns had healed, leaving only faint scars.

It was a fabulous day, still winter but with the promise of spring in the air. The seabirds flew screaming over them as they splashed through the shallow water at the edge of the beach.

Kelsie looked out at the dark green islands dotting the sparkling blue cove. The air smelled salty and fresh-washed from spring rains. On her left the town of Dark Cove rose from the beachfront. Small houses painted red, blue and green stood out against the gray rocks. Halfway up the steep hill the Clam Shack, with a bright new sign swinging in the wind, perched like a white gull on a rock. This is the best reward of all, thought Kelsie. I'm home.

"I'll race you!" she called back to Jen.

About the Author ⊚

Sharon Siamon was born in Saskatoon, Saskatchewan, in the year of the horse. Crazy about horses since she was old enough to say "horse," Sharon began riding, like many of her readers, by borrowing a friend's horse. She read every horse book she could get her hands on and now writes them for young readers who share her love of horses.

Her first books, *Gallop for Gold* and *A Horse for Josie Moon*, are set in northern Ontario where Sharon, her husband and three daughters built a log cabin. Her popular Mustang Mountain books—with a million books in print worldwide—are set in the Alberta mountain wilderness where she loves to ride. Inspiration for her new Saddle Island series came from seeing a beautiful white horse galloping along Nova Scotia's Atlantic shore. Along with horses, Sharon loves the ocean—maybe because she's a Pisces, the sign of the fish.

ISBN 1-55285-713-1   ISBN 1-55285-714-X

Set on Nova Scotia's wild and windswept eastern shore, the first instalment in this series, *Gallop to the Sea*, introduces the spirited Kelsie, as she tries to rescue a rebellious horse named Caspar. Kelsie plans to swim Caspar to a mysterious deserted island before his owner ships him off for auction.

A violent storm develops, putting Kelsie and Caspar in great danger. Will they make it to shore safely? This first adventure from Saddle Island puts readers in the thick of intrigue and adventure.

In *Secrets in the Sand*, Kelsie MacKay has a problem. She has a chance to add three more horses to her Saddle Island refuge, but there's no money to keep them. Kelsie's counting on the rich stranger from Boston to change her Aunt Maggie's mind. Her brother Andy is banking on finding treasure on Saddle Island to get them out of their money fix.

But Saddle Island doesn't give up its secrets easily. Wild winds, tides and dangerous rocks threaten Kelsie, Andy and their friend Jen. Can they escape, and will Kelsie and Andy find a way to keep the horses and stay in Dark Cove?